DATE DUE			
May 13		1997	12-20

THE DISAPPEARING BIKE SHOP

BIKE SHOP

✹✹✹✹✹✹

Elvira Woodruff

Holiday House / New York

Copyright © 1992 by Elvira Woodruff
ALL RIGHTS RESERVED
Printed in the United States of America
FIRST EDITION

Library of Congress Cataloging-in-Publication Data
Woodruff, Elvira.
The disappearing bike shop / by Elvira Woodruff.
p.   cm.
Summary: *Fifth graders Freckle and Tyler meet an unusual bicycle*
salesman and inventor who turns out to be Leonardo da Vinci,
traveling through time.
ISBN 0-8234-0933-3
1. *Leonardo, da Vinci, 1452–1519—Juvenile fiction.*
[1. *Leonardo, da Vinci, 1452–1519—Fiction.   2. Time travel—*
Fiction.   3. Science fiction.]   I. Title.
PZ7.W8606Di   1992   91-29863   CIP   AC
[Fic]—dc20

For my cousin, Frank Asch,
in whose footsteps I've tried to follow,
but alas the boy's feet are just too big

CHAPTER ONE

"Hey, Freck, come look at this," Tyler Harrison called. He was pointing to a crimson-leafed tree that arched over the sidewalk. "There's a little green feather caught in those branches. I wonder where it came from?"

"Who cares?" Freckle shrugged.

Freckle Kosa was Tyler's best friend. His real name was Jay, but since he had more than three hundred freckles on his face alone (Tyler had counted them one day), it was difficult to call him anything but Freckle. (Even his mother called him that.)

Freckle looked up at the clouds hanging over Dewberry Street. A few drops of rain were beginning to fall. "If we're going to make it home before the storm," he said, "you can't keep stopping to look at a million different things. Who cares about some old feather anyway?"

"I do," Tyler said, stretching his neck. He was almost a full head shorter than Freckle, although both boys were in the same fifth-grade class. Tyler pushed his straight black hair away from his eyes and looked at his friend. "I want to find out where things come from and why they're the way they are. That way I can be a world-famous scientist someday."

"I thought you wanted to be a world-famous inventor. That's what you said last week," Freckle reminded him, as they continued pushing their bicycles down the sidewalk. "And the week before that you wanted to be a world-famous pizza maker, remember?"

"I don't have to be just one thing, you know," Tyler said. "There are all kinds of things I could be when I grow up."

"Maybe you could be a world-famous cookie maker and give my mom some lessons. She's into 'healthful snacks' lately. She can't make a cookie anymore without putting gross stuff in it, like figs and dates and prunes."

"Prunes aren't so bad," Tyler said.

"They aren't?" Freckle exclaimed. "Are we talking about the same black slimy wrinkled little balls that start with *P* and end with *E*?"

"I sort of like prunes," Tyler admitted.

"On second thought, maybe you should forget about the cookie-making business," Freckle suggested. "You should become a world-famous bicycle repairman instead." He nodded toward Tyler's bicycle. "Then if your chain broke, you could take out a repair kit and fix your bike on the spot, instead of having to push it all the way home."

"I can't believe my chain broke." Tyler sighed, looking down at his bicycle. "I'll probably have to wait until Saturday for my mom to take me to the bike shop at the mall to get another one." He glanced at Freckle and frowned. "You don't have to walk with me if you don't want to."

"That's OK," Freckle said, his face softening into a smile. "I'll stay with you as long as you don't keep stopping every second."

Tyler didn't answer. He had stopped again and was looking down at a little seedling that was growing out of the sidewalk.

"Now what are you looking at?" Freckle groaned.

"Wow, look, Freck. This little tree is growing right through the crack in the cement," Tyler replied, bending over the seedling. "I wonder how that happened. I guess a bird could have dropped the seed, or maybe the wind blew it there."

"Wow, that's amazing, really the most amazing thing I've ever seen." Freckle smirked. "And look at this, my shoelace is untied. I wonder how that happened? Maybe a bird untied it or maybe it was the wind. Why don't we just stand here for another hour and try to figure it out?"

"OK, OK, I'm moving," Tyler said, straightening up. But he hadn't taken more than a few steps, when he stopped again.

"Now what?" Freckle moaned, coming up behind him. "What's so amazing this time? Another feather? A baby tree? What?"

"Tha . . . tha . . . that!" Tyler stammered, pointing down the street. Freckle followed his gaze and both boys stood staring at the most amazing thing they had ever seen. It was an old building at the far end of Dewberry Street.

The front of the building was like many of the other storefronts in town. It had a gabled roof, a brick front, and a big display window. However, unlike the other brick-and-clapboard structures on the street, this old storefront was attached to an ancient-looking stone building. But there was something even more unusual. The building was breaking loose from its foundation and slowly rising in the air!

"I don't believe it!" Freckle gasped. "I see it, but I don't believe it!"

"Look, it's . . . it's . . . beginning to disappear!" Tyler whispered. As the two watched, a loud hissing noise filled the air. The big display window began to grow cloudy, and the pointed gabled roof began to fade. Brick by brick, stone by stone, the whole building was disappearing! Within seconds the entire structure had vanished, invisibly wrenched from its stone foundation, sucked into a whirling cloud of dust.

Freckle let out a faint cry and stepped backward, while Tyler bit down on his lip and took a step forward.

CHAPTER TWO

"Where are you going?" Freckle cried as Tyler wheeled his bicycle down the sidewalk toward the empty lot.

"We've got to find out what's going on, don't we?" Tyler answered.

"We've got to call the police, that's what we've got to do," Freckle yelled. "When a person sees a building lift off the ground and then disappear, he should call the police."

"But, Freck, what can the police do? They'll just search for clues, which is something we can do. Don't you want to investigate? We're the first ones at the scene of the crime, that is, if a disappearing building is a crime. Maybe someday we could be world-famous investigators."

"Ty, this is serious," Freckle said. "It's like

black magic or something. We should call someone, a grown-up, or your brother, Lee. Something bad could happen to us. I'm scared."

"I'm scared too," Tyler admitted. "But the building is gone, and an empty lot can't hurt us. Besides, Lee would never believe that we saw a building disappear, and he'd probably call us babies, if we let him know we were scared. Come on, Freck, maybe we can find some clues."

Freckle didn't budge. "I'm not risking my life to look for clues," he grumbled.

"You know how you've always wanted to be on TV," Tyler called over his shoulder. "Well, if we discover some clues and then take them to the police, I bet you anything they'll put us on the evening news."

Freckle decided it might be worth risking his life to get on TV. He began to follow Tyler. When they reached the empty lot, the two boys leaned their bicycles against the stone foundation.

"I wonder where it went?" Tyler whispered, as he ran his fingers over the rough stone.

"I don't know," Freckle whispered back. "I

didn't think things could really disappear." A loud hissing noise suddenly filled the air, and both boys looked up to see a large billowing cloud of dust spinning over their heads.

"Oh, no, Ty," Freckle screamed, "it's coming back! It's coming back!"

"Quick, get behind that tree," Tyler yelled, running across the street. As he and Freckle raced for cover, the hissing noise grew louder and louder. They peeked around the trunk. They could see that the old building was reappearing on the empty lot. It stood trembling and shaking, a few feet above the ground. Then it settled into place in a cloud of dust.

"Let's get out of here," Freckle whimpered.

"OK," Tyler agreed breathlessly. "But what about our bikes?" Their bicycles were still leaning against the old stone foundation.

"I told you we should have called the police," Freckle moaned.

"Well, we can't leave our bikes here. They might disappear with the building. My dad gave me that bike. I can't lose it," Tyler said. "Let's wait for a while and see what happens." They crouched down behind the tree, waiting and watching, for what seemed like hours.

"Come on, Freck," Tyler finally said, "I don't think that building is going anywhere. We'll just grab the bikes and get out of here as fast as we can." He pulled Freckle by the sleeve, and the two boys stepped out from behind the tree. Clinging to each other, they crossed the street to the building. Freckle grabbed his bicycle and turned to leave, but Tyler's curiosity was getting the better of him.

"I wonder what's in this store, anyway," he mumbled, pressing his face to the glass window. "Wow, it's a bike shop! Freck, come see," he said.

As Freckle stepped up to the glass, Tyler pointed to a large red and silver unicycle inside the shop. It was next to an old-fashioned bicycle, with sleigh runners attached to the front and back wheels.

"It must be for riding on ice," Freckle exclaimed. An unusual-looking tricycle stood behind it, with three big wheels, and a little wooden cart attached to the rear fender. It was painted shiny black and plated with gleaming nickel.

"I've never seen a bike shop like this before," Tyler exclaimed, his eyes traveling around the store. Old-fashioned oil lamps hung from ornate brass brackets on the walls, bathing everything in a warm amber glow. Outside, along Dewberry Street, storm clouds raced overhead, making the scene within seem all the more unreal.

"Look, there's a parrot!" Freckle gasped, pointing to a brightly colored bird that had flown down from a shelf. The parrot's brilliant green and red feathers fanned out dramatically, and his turquoise-colored eyes shone in the lamplight as he perched on a silver three-wheeler. Both boys stood transfixed, unable to move from the window.

"I bet the green feather in the tree came from that parrot," Tyler whispered. "He must live in this bike shop."

"The bike shop at the mall sure doesn't look anything like this," Freckle exclaimed.

"This is like something out of a dream!" Tyler murmured. He watched as the parrot flew to a counter at the back of the store, where an old man sat. He was wearing a worn brown leather apron, and his balding head was bent over a large book. Six fat honey-colored candles were burning in a wheel suspended from the ceiling above him. The parrot glided under the wheel and landed on his shoulder. The old man's eyes twinkled mysteriously in the candlelight as he looked up and smiled. Both boys gasped in fright.

"He must be the one who made the building disappear," Freckle croaked, backing away from the window. "He must be a wizard or something. Did you see what the back of the building looked like, when it was in the air? It was huge. That old man is probably a wizard. Let's get out of here, now."

"Wait," Tyler cried. "Look at that sign." He pointed to the green-and-gold sign that hung over the door. It said:

QUIGLEY'S BICYCLE SHOP

REPAIRS, SUNDRIES . . . AND MORE

QUENTIN QUIGLEY, PROPRIETOR

A small wooden bicycle wheel hung from the sign.

"I wonder what sundries are," Tyler muttered.

"Who cares, let's get out of here," Freckle pleaded.

"Look at the writing on the wheel," Tyler
said. "It says 'The Wheel of Time Waits for No
Man.' What do you suppose that means?" Suddenly the figure of the old man appeared at the
display window. Both boys let out a yelp and
turned their bicycles around. As they started
up the sidewalk, Tyler could hear the tinkling
of bells. He turned around to see the door to
Quigley's Bicycle Shop creak open and the
brilliant-colored parrot fly out. Tyler's mouth
dropped open as he watched the bird fly above
them. Then with a loud squawk, it swooped
down and landed on Freckle's head!

CHAPTER THREE

Freckle's eyes bugged out and the tips of his ears turned a bright red. He looked like he was about to cry.

Suddenly, as if by magic, the old man appeared beside them. Tyler was so startled, he jumped back, bumping into Freckle, which set the parrot to squawking. "Found a nice nest . . . eee . . . found a nice nest . . ." Freckle closed his eyes as the bird flapped his wings noisily.

Tyler stared at the strange old man, who was wearing a long green robe that dropped to the ground. It was trimmed in gold thread and belted at the waist with a crimson cord. The worn leather apron hung down in front, with the initials Q.Q. stitched in black thread in the lower left-hand corner.

This must be Quentin Quigley, Tyler was thinking. And he does look like a wizard! It's not just his robe. It's the way he has his hair tied in a ponytail, and that long silver beard. It reminded Tyler of the pictures he had seen of wizards in books. Tyler looked into the old man's eyes. They were a deep brown, almost black. But they weren't the eyes of a grown-up. They seemed more like the eyes of a child, opened wide with a look of surprise. A shiver ran through Tyler as the old man began to speak.

"Ah, Verrocchio, come *bella mia.*" The wizard held out his hand, and the parrot flew to him, perching on his outstretched finger.

He sounds like he's from another country, Tyler thought. But it wasn't just the old man's accent and foreign words that made his speech seem strange. His voice had a harmonic quality. When he spoke, it was like music, strange and beautiful music from another age.

"I couldn't help noticing that you both have bicycles. Are they in need of repair? Perhaps Quigley's could be of service," the old man said. He bent down and ran his bony finger up and down the rim of Tyler's wheel. "Ah, yes, little one, your chain is broken. Leave it at Quigley's. We can repair it."

"Bu . . . but . . . I don't have any money to pay for it," Tyler stammered as the old man took the bicycle from him and began wheeling it toward the shop.

"You're not to worry." The old man grinned, his eyes lighting up as he looked at them over his shoulder. "Since we're new in this location, and you're our first customer, I think we can agree on a trade. Come into the shop now, it's starting to rain." He pushed Tyler's bicycle through the open door. Verrocchio flew in after him. Tyler and Freckle stood outside on the sidewalk, not knowing what to do next.

"Are you crazy?" Freckle gasped as Tyler took a step forward. "You're not really going in there, are you?"

"I have to," Tyler told him. "He's got my bike. Does Mr. Quigley look like a wizard to you?" he asked.

"Yes," Freckle agreed. "And the way that building disappeared, I'd say he's got some powerful magic. If we go in there, he'll probably cast a spell and turn us into frogs or toads. I wouldn't be surprised if that old parrot wasn't a person at one time. He was probably some poor kid who just wanted to get a bike chain fixed, like you do, and now look at him!"

"Freckle, this is real life, not a fairy tale." Tyler shook his head, gazing again at the sign above the door. "What do you suppose he wants to trade his work for?"

"Probably your soul!" Freckle wailed. "Do you remember that story Mrs. Bailey read us about the devil who traded a bunch of money to a man for his soul?"

"He's just fixing my chain. He's not the devil." Tyler sighed.

"So how do you explain the building disappearing?" Freckle wanted to know.

"I'm not sure." Tyler frowned. "Maybe Mr. Quigley is some kind of scientist or something, and he's created some kind of energy that can make things disappear."

"If he's a scientist, he's a mad scientist," Freckle said. "Did you see the way he was dressed in that old bathrobe and those pointed slippers?"

"I know he's weird, but I don't think he's evil or anything," Tyler said. "There's something nice about him. Don't you want to find out what is going on? How could he make that building disappear? Come on, Freck, we have to go back in," he said. "Besides, I have to get my bike back, and I wouldn't let you go in alone if it were your bike."

"What if we disappear along with the building?" Freckle moaned. "And what if that big old parrot decides to make a nest in my hair again?" he muttered, running his hand through his blond curls.

"If we see the place starting to disappear, we'll just run out the door. I'm sure Mr. Quigley won't let his parrot land on you again. Don't worry," Tyler told him. It was beginning to rain harder. There was no awning on the building and no place for shelter, except in the store.

"Come on, Freck, we can't stay out here or we'll get soaked," Tyler yelled. He went up to the half-closed door. Freckle reluctantly followed.

"I think we're making a big mistake, Ty," Freckle said. "I still think we should call the poli . . ." but his voice was lost in the tinkling of bells overhead as Tyler pushed the door all the way open. The wide oak floorboards creaked under the boys' sneakers. They could smell kerosene mixed with the warm sweet scent of leather. The lamplights flickered as bicycle wheels spun gently overhead. The whole room twinkled with the sparkle of chrome and nickel.

"Look at the label on this bike," Tyler gasped, pointing to a cherry-red unicycle that stood by the door. "It says, 'Winston Bicycle Company, 1894.' Do you think this bike could really be that old?"

"Amazing, absolutely amazing!" a voice suddenly exclaimed. Both boys turned to see the old man standing near the display window, staring at a plane that was flying in the distance.

"Amazing, absolutely amazing!" he mumbled again, with a shake of his head.

"What does he think is so amazing?" Freckle asked.

"I don't know, maybe it doesn't rain much in his country." Tyler took a few steps over to the window. "Uh . . . excuse me, Mr. Quigley, but, uh . . . well I was wondering about my bike."

"Ah, yes." The old man smiled as he looked

down at Tyler's bicycle. "Incredible, the over-all design hasn't changed all that much," he said.

"Do you think that you can fix it?" Tyler croaked, pointing to the broken chain.

"In what year was this bicycle made?" the old man asked.

"What year? Uh . . . well, my dad bought it for me for my last birthday so I guess it was made last year," Tyler told him.

"And this year?" The old man's eyes were twinkling and his lips were curling into a smile. "Will you tell me what year it is now?"

Tyler stole a glance at Freckle, who looked as puzzled as he did.

"Why it's . . . it's 1992, of course," Tyler said.

"Ah! 1992! Incredible!" The old man threw back his head and laughed.

"I guess you're feeling a little confused to-day." Tyler tried to smile. "My great-grandpa gets like that sometimes. It's OK," he said, turning his bicycle around. "We'll just come back another time." But before he could take another step, the old man put his hand on Tyler's shoulder.

"Nonsense," he said softly, as Verrocchio began to squawk. "I would be glad to make the necessary repairs. Please forgive my memory lapse, it is nothing but an old man's foolishness. The mind plays tricks. Come back tomorrow, and I promise I will have your bicycle . . ." BANG! The old man was suddenly interrupted by a loud noise, like a gunshot, coming from behind the curtain.

"What was that?" Freckle asked.

"It sounded like a gunshot," Tyler said, as a wave of goose bumps ran down his arms.

"Ah, my sheep bladder," the old man mumbled, disappearing behind the curtain.

"Let's get out of here while we still can," Freckle cried.

"Did he say there's a sheep back there?" Tyler asked. Before Freckle could answer, the old man had popped his head back out from behind the curtain, his long silver beard falling over the deep red velvet material.

"Is everything all right, Mr. Quigley?" Tyler asked. "Did anyone get hurt? Did you say you had a sheep back there?"

The old man cocked his head and smiled.

"Yes, everything is fine. And, no, I don't have a whole sheep, just part of it."

"Part of it?" Tyler asked.

The old man nodded his head. "Yes, a sheep's bladder is made of very elastic material. If you fill it with air, using a bellows, the bladder can be expanded to amazing dimensions, to the size of this room, for instance. Eventually, however, the material is stretched so thin that it breaks, as one did just now. I've yet to discover the breaking point. Ah, there is so much to discover about this world of ours."

"I guess there is," Tyler agreed, as he and Freckle inched their way to the door. "I never even thought about a sheep's bladder before."

"Um, it's an amazing world," the old man mumbled. "Full of incredible things like a sheep's bladder, moonlight, and rainbows. Have you ever dreamt of making a rainbow?" he asked.

"A rainbow?" Tyler repeated aloud.

"Yes, I would say the creation of a rainbow is a thing worthy of our dreams. Ah, to dream, that is the miracle, but I ramble on. You will have to beg my pardon," he apologized. "Do come back tomorrow and we will see about that bicycle of yours." He parted the curtain and with his long wrinkled fingers, he waved good-bye.

Tyler and Freckle nervously waved back, then hurried for the door. Before they could open it, however, Verrocchio let out a piercing squawk.

"Keep the shop a secret . . . eee . . . keep the shop a secret . . . eeee."

"Yes, my friends," the old man called to them, his expression suddenly turning serious, "Verrocchio is quite right to remind me. We are not quite ready for our grand opening in this new location, so Quigley's Bicycle Shop must be our private secret. No one else is to know about it. Do you understand?" Tyler felt the power of his gaze. It was almost hypnotic. "You will promise to keep the shop a secret, won't you?"

"Yes, we'll keep the secret," Tyler managed to say.

"Very good, my friends." The old man smiled. "I look forward to seeing you tomorrow."

CHAPTER FOUR

"We actually made it out alive," said Freckle, once they were on the sidewalk. The rain had stopped and the scent of wet leaves hung on the cool autumn breeze. "I don't get it," he continued. "I don't get anything about this place." He reached for his bicycle and started pedaling. Tyler ran beside him.

"We can ask Mr. Quigley more questions tomorrow," Tyler said.

"We? *We* can ask him?" Freckle cried. "Make that you. You can ask him, because I'm never going back there. He can make the building disappear, and did you hear all that stuff about a sheep's bladder? Sounds like some kind of voodoo wizard stuff to me. I'm not going anywhere near him and his old Verrolio."

"Verrocchio," Tyler corrected him.

"Oh, who cares what his name is!" Freckle snapped. "The old guy is definitely some kind of wizard or something, and I'm telling you, it isn't safe to go back there."

"Freckle, even if he is a wizard, he's a nice wizard. He likes us, and I don't think he would hurt us." Tyler tried to reassure him.

"You can't be sure of that," Freckle said, shaking his head. "Why haven't we ever seen that building before? And isn't the end of Dewberry Street a weird place to set up a new business? No one comes this far down the street but us. I wonder what he's up to?"

Tyler chewed on his lower lip. He knew Freckle was right. No one ever came this far down Dewberry Street, since there were so many empty buildings. The only reason he and Freckle biked home this way was because it was a shortcut to the alley behind Carlton Street, where they lived.

Where did Mr. Quigley come from? Tyler was thinking. And what kind of power did he really have? He certainly looked like a wizard.

"Just wait till we tell the guys at school tomorrow." Freckle interrupted his thoughts. "Do you realize, this is the best story anybody's had all year? They'll never believe it! Especially the disappearing part." The two boys had reached the alley and were dodging the puddles.

"We can't tell anyone!" Tyler exclaimed. "I promised Mr. Quigley that we wouldn't tell anyone about the shop, not yet, anyway."

"Oh, come on, Tyler," Freckle pleaded. "You know how Frankie G. always has the best stories. You've got to let me at least tell Frankie."

Tyler shook his head no. "We just can't. Not now," he said. "If the old man is powerful enough to make buildings disappear, just imagine what he could do to us if he found out we went back on our promise."

"Why did you have to make a promise, anyway?" Freckle groaned. "Didn't your mother ever tell you about not taking candy from strangers or making promises to wizards?"

Tyler grinned. "I know Mr. Quigley is strange and the whole thing is scary," he admitted. "But there's just something about him and his shop, something special, you know?"

"It is the most incredible bike shop in town," Freckle admitted.

"In town?" Tyler exclaimed, jumping over a large puddle. "Freck, Quigley's Bicycle Shop is probably the most incredible bike shop in the world! And that's another reason why we have to keep it a secret for now. Don't you see? It's like our own special place that no one else knows about. Hey, I've got an idea." He stopped walking for a second. "We could start a secret club. Only the members of the club would know the secret."

"And that means only us," remarked Freckle. "But then the club would have just two members. Isn't that kind of dumb?"

"What's wrong with two members?" Tyler said. "I think it's neat, like a secret society."

The wind picked up as the two boys left the alley and headed toward Carlton Street. Soon they were walking in the shadows of the old evergreen trees that lined the paths of the park. The fresh aroma of wet pine needles filled the air. Tyler took a deep breath and shivered as he looked up at the towering fir trees. He loved this part of the park. It was almost like being lost in the woods, with the trees dark and stately and filled with mystery. He was thinking how the ancient evergreens reminded him of people, old mysterious people. It was then that he thought of Quentin Quigley.

He's like one of these old trees, Tyler decided, as his eyes traveled up the branches. He stood gazing at the sky, just above the tree line, when there suddenly appeared the biggest, most beautiful rainbow he had ever seen. Its soft-hued arc swung directly over his head and into the park. As Tyler followed the glorious line of color, his eyes grew wide with wonder.

"Oh, my gosh," Tyler gasped. "Look! Look where it's coming from!" The magnificent rainbow seemed to be coming from the far end of Dewberry Street.

CHAPTER FIVE

I wonder if Mr. Quigley made that rainbow, Tyler thought as he lay in bed that night, gazing out his window at the star-sprinkled sky. And if Mr. Quigley can make buildings disappear, he can probably make rainbows too. Tyler snuggled against his pillow and tried closing his eyes. It took him a long time to fall asleep. When he finally did, he had the strangest dream.

He dreamt that he and Freckle were on a bicycle built for two, and they were riding straight into a rainbow. In the dream Tyler heard his friend calling, but when Tyler turned around, Freckle had changed into a parrot. A big fat parrot with freckles all over his green feathers!

"Eeee . . . eee, Freckle want a cracker . . .

Freckle want some prune crackers, eee," Freckle the parrot screeched. Tyler sat on the bike, bewildered.

"But, Freck," he called back to the parrot, "you don't even like prunes!"

When Tyler's mother came to wake him for school the next morning, Tyler was already up and getting dressed. He was thinking about his strange dream as he pulled his sweatshirt over his head.

"My goodness," his mother exclaimed, "you're certainly in a hurry to start the day! Is there something special going on at school?"

"No," Tyler said, shaking his head, "just the usual stuff." He wished he could tell his mother about Mr. Quigley and his shop, but he remembered his promise. He wondered if the secret would still be safe if he only told his family. He was dying to tell somebody.

"I'm sorry I got in so late last night," his mother said. "This new computer class is rough, and I stayed late for some extra help. I'm so glad Lee is old enough to get you two supper on my class nights." She had carried a pile of clean clothes over to Tyler's dresser and was putting them away.

If Mom asks me what I did after school yesterday, Tyler thought, I can't lie to her. Kids
aren't supposed to lie to their mothers. He sat,
half hoping that his mother would ask, but she
didn't. She was in a hurry to get dressed for
work, and after she finished putting away the
clothes, she rushed out the door and disappeared into her bedroom. Ever since Tyler's
parents had gotten divorced two years ago, his
mother always was rushing, either to work, or
to shop, or to meet with friends. And recently
she had begun dating. She would rush off to
meet "Mr. Wrong." Actually the man's name
was Richard, but one day, Lee and Tyler had
overheard their mother call him "Mr. Right."
Since then they'd nicknamed him Mr. Wrong.
They didn't like Richard.

Tyler went into the kitchen and found Lee
at the table, listening to a tape on his headphones, while he ate his breakfast and finished
his homework.

I wonder what Lee would say if he heard
about Quigley's Bicycle Shop, Tyler wondered
as he watched his big brother shovel some cereal into his mouth. Lee's bowl was sur-

rounded by schoolbooks and homework papers. Every now and then he would put down his spoon and pick up a pen to finish a map that he was working on for history. Tyler wished Lee would look at him and say something. He still wanted to keep his promise to Mr. Quigley, but maybe telling a big brother wouldn't count.

"That looks cool," Tyler said, pointing to Lee's map, hoping to get his attention. But Lee kept his head bent over his work, nodding every now and then to the song that he was listening to on his headphones. Tyler shrugged.

"But not as cool as what I saw yesterday," he continued, pouring some cereal into a bowl. "I saw a rainbow and I met the person who made the rainbow."

"I wish I could get your love," Lee croaked out of tune, as his tape played on.

"I wish you could get a voice," Tyler groaned, holding his hands over his ears. Ever since Lee had turned thirteen, he had begun to wear his headphones wherever he went. He looked up at Tyler and back down at his map, bobbing his head up and down to the music as he continued to sing, draw, and eat, all at the same time.

"I bet you never met anybody that could make a rainbow," Tyler continued, staring across the table.

"What did you say about a rainbow?" his mother asked as she came into the kitchen.

"Uh . . . I was just talking about a rainbow that I saw yesterday on my way home from school," Tyler mumbled.

"Oh, yes, it must have been the same rainbow that I saw," his mother said excitedly. "Was it over the park at around four o'clock?"

Tyler gulped. Here it was. She was asking, wasn't she? He had to answer. A wave of relief washed over him. He found himself suddenly ready to tell her everything. "Yes, that's the one," he said. "And I know the person who . . ."

"You know," his mother interrupted, "Richard called me at work from his office at the courthouse and told me to look out my window. If he hadn't called I would have missed it. Richard says that rainbows are good luck, and that if you point a rainbow out to someone else, you get double the luck. I never heard that before." His mother smiled, a dreamy look coming over her face. Then she blinked and looked at Tyler, as if she suddenly noticed that he was in the same room. "I'm sorry, what were you saying, Ty?"

"Nothing," Tyler muttered, shoving a spoonful of cereal into his mouth. Why did she have to go and ruin a perfectly good rainbow story by sticking Mr. Wrong into it? Tyler ate the rest of his cereal in silence. He wouldn't tell her now. He couldn't.

She probably wouldn't hear a word I said, anyway, he decided. She's got the dopey look on her face she gets whenever she talks about Mr. Wrong. Tyler looked over at his brother. And Lee is too busy croaking to some dopey love song, so I won't tell him either. Tyler got up from the table. He suddenly felt all alone. Having a secret wasn't easy, he discovered, especially when you tried to tell everyone and no one listened!

CHAPTER SIX

As Tyler walked over to Freckle's house that morning, his mood began to change. He started to feel better as he thought about the bicycle shop. He hoped that Freckle would want to stop and visit Mr. Quigley on the way to school.

Tyler smiled, and waved to Freckle, who was coming down the walk with his flute case. Both boys had decided that it would be fun to learn an instrument, so they had signed up for flute lessons at the beginning of the year. Mr. Schocker, the school's music teacher, gave them their lesson in school on Tuesdays.

"Hey, little Tyler Tidy Wipe," a voice suddenly called from across the street. It was Michael Beidelman, otherwise known as the

Viking, or Mike the Vike, or just plain Vike. He was the class bully, and he was always picking on boys who were smaller than he was. Unfortunately Tyler was the smallest boy in the fourth grade, while the Viking was one of the biggest. He had big broad shoulders, long arms, and big hands with red knuckles. Everything about him was big, even his teeth. His straw-colored hair shot out in zigzags from under a green-and-orange baseball cap that always sat backward on his head. Whenever Tyler saw Michael Beidelman, he thought of the pictures of Vikings in his history book. Michael Beidelman's nickname couldn't have suited him more.

Just my luck to have a Viking living two streets away from me, Tyler thought, as he watched Michael Beidelman walk up to a group of second and third graders.

"Going to play us a little tune on your little toy flute, Tidy Wipe?" the Viking yelled from across the street. Tyler's stomach tightened into a knot as he heard the second and third graders begin to laugh.

"Vike, were you talking to us?" Freckle

yelled back. He stepped off the curb and hurried across the street. Freckle was just as tall as the Viking and almost as broad shouldered.

I'd give anything to be able to do that, Tyler thought as he watched Freckle stare down the Viking. I'm only as big as the second graders, he thought miserably. And they're only seven and eight years old! He dug his hands into his pockets as he caught the eye of one of the second graders. The boy was staring at him. Tyler's cheeks burned with shame. His breath came in short angry puffs. Part of him was glad that Freckle was there to defend him, but another part of him, a bigger part, was ashamed and angry that he needed Freckle at all. He stood gritting his teeth, waiting for it to be over.

It didn't take long, for the Viking was speechless at the prospect of having to deal with someone his own size. Freckle finally backed away from him. But with an audience of younger boys still surrounding him, the bully couldn't resist one last taunt. He waited until Freckle had crossed back to Tyler's side of the street, then yelled out, "Hey, little Tidy

Wipe, if you need to find your kindergarten classroom, just ask the second graders. They'll show you the way."

"I'll show him where he belongs," Freckle huffed.

Tyler reached over and grabbed his sweatshirt. "Don't," he said, holding onto Freckle's arm. He didn't want his friend to have to stand up for him again. Tyler's face was crimson now as he began to tremble with anger. He turned his head and looked across the street. "You think you're so big," he yelled as loud as he could. "But you're just a big worm. The biggest worm on Wormwood Avenue." All the second and third graders laughed, for everyone knew that the Viking lived on Wormwood Avenue. The Viking's face turned beet red and little spit bubbles came out of his mouth. He began to sputter something that no one could hear.

"The worm on Wormwood Avenue, that was pretty good." Freckle grinned. Tyler smiled too. He knew he could never have said such a thing if Freckle hadn't been standing beside him, but it did feel like a victory of sorts. He stole a glance across the street. The Viking made a fist and held it up. Tyler quickly looked away.

"He's such a big wimp," Freckle said. "He only picks on the smallest kids. Uh, no offense, Ty. You may be the shortest kid in our class, but you've definitely got the biggest brain."

"Well, my big brain is telling me that we had better postpone our mission," Tyler whispered.

"Our mission?" Freckle looked confused.

"I wanted to turn up Dewberry Street this morning, but we can't now that the Viking is following us. We can check it out after school."

"Dewberry Street?" Freckle moaned. "Oh, Ty, I was hoping you'd change your mind about going back there. That whole thing was like a bad dream."

"You want to be in the club, don't you?" Tyler asked as he turned to look at the Viking, who was still on the other side of the street.

Freckle hesitated. "Yeah, I guess so."

"Then we've got to go back and check out the shop," Tyler said firmly. "Besides, I've got to get my bike and I want to ask about the building disappearing and how Mr. Quigley made that rainbow." Tyler looked at Freckle and grinned. "We can call this mission 'The Rainbow Mission.'"

"Why don't we just call it the Voodoo Black Magic Sheep Bladder Mission?" Freckle winced. "We can find out about that too, while we're there. You know, I asked my dad if he ever heard of anyone blowing up a sheep's bladder, and he thought I was joking."

"Freck, I told you Quigley's Bicycle Shop is our private secret," Tyler exclaimed. "You didn't tell your dad or anyone else about it, did you?" Freckle suddenly had a strange expression on his face.

"Freckle Kosa, you didn't!" Tyler cried. "Who did you tell?"

"Just one person," Freckle muttered in a small guilty voice. "Just my little sister Shelly."

"How could you?" Tyler cried, forgetting for a moment that he had almost broken the promise himself.

"I just had to tell somebody," Freckle tried to explain. "Besides, she's only in kindergarten. And you know how she's always making up stuff. At the supper table last night she told my parents that she couldn't eat her carrots because carrots give her hiccups. Then she said she couldn't eat her peas because they make her talk in her sleep, and if she talked in her sleep, the two ponies who live in her bedroom closet would wake up and start kicking on the closet door."

"She's got two ponies living in her bedroom closet?" Tyler looked confused.

"No, of course she doesn't." Freckle sighed. "She just pretends that she does. And she told my parents that she didn't want her ponies waking everyone up, so she wasn't going to eat her peas. Everyone knows that she hates peas. So you don't have to worry about Shelly, because even if she did start talking about a building disappearing and a wizard, who's going to believe her?"

"OK, I guess the secret's safe, but you have to swear not to tell anyone else," Tyler said firmly as they crossed the street.

"I swear," Freckle agreed. "But what if old man Quigley casts a spell on us and turns us into frogs or something? How will our parents ever find us?"

"Even if he is a wizard," Tyler said, shaking his head, "do you know how much power he'd have to have to turn a person into a frog?"

"About as much power as it takes to make a building disappear," Freckle whispered.

CHAPTER SEVEN

Tyler and Freckle ran around the playground twice before the first bell rang. Once settled into their seats in Mrs. Bailey's fourth-grade class, they spent most of the morning passing notes back and forth. Tyler looked down at the note Freckle had passed to him. On the outside of the paper Freckle had scribbled Top Secreet. Tyler knew Freckle's spelling was not the best, but he was glad to see that his friend had gotten into the spirit of things.

The two boys were careful not to let the notes get into anyone else's hands. Tyler became more careless, however, as the morning dragged on. He could barely concentrate on the science reports that some of the kids were delivering in Mrs. Bailey's class. Tom Buckley was giving his report on birds. He had just told the class that the turkey vulture defends itself by vomiting on its enemies. Tyler could hear everyone laughing and then he heard a familiar growl.

"Top Secret, is it?" the Viking sneered, picking up one of the notes Tyler had passed to Freckle. Freckle had gone to the boys' room. Tyler jumped out of his seat and tried to stop the Viking from reading the note, but it was too late. He had already opened it and read the message, "After school prepare for the Rainbow Mission."

"Ooooo, the Rainbow Mission," he whispered with a grin.

"Give me back my note," Tyler demanded.

"Who's going to make me?" the Viking asked, crumpling the note in his hand and stuffing it into his pocket. Tyler's face grew hot as he heard Danny Featherman and Marc Freer begin to snicker behind him. He knew everyone was watching, including Mrs. Bailey. She frowned. "We don't need you two boys creating any problems. Take your seat, Tyler, and get back to work," she said firmly (so firmly that Tyler didn't hesitate and quickly returned to his seat). His face burned with embarrassment. He looked at Freckle as he came back into the room. Why did you have to go and leave the note on your desk? he thought. What a stupid thing to do! Did you hear that? A stupid thing to do! Tyler was concentrating as hard as he could, hoping that Freckle would read his mind, but Freckle didn't appear to be reading anything. He stood staring down at the floor. He didn't look very well. His eyelids were heavy, his face was flushed, and even his freckles looked pink. Freckle's mouth twisted in pain as he held his hand to his throat. Tyler watched as he slowly made his way over to Mrs. Bailey's desk.

"What's wrong, Jay?" Mrs. Bailey asked. "Don't you feel well?"

"No," Freckle moaned. "My throat really hurts, it's hard to swallow, and my head hurts."

Mrs. Bailey put her hand on his forehead and shook her head. "You do feel warm. I want you to go to the nurse at once."

Freckle looked over at Tyler and waved limply as he walked out of the room. For the rest of the science class, Tyler sat staring at the door, waiting for his friend's return. By the time the class had moved on to social studies, though, his worst fear had come true. The nurse had called on the intercom, asking for Freckle's things to be sent to her office. He was going home.

"Abby, you can help me collect Jay's things and take them to the nurse's office," Mrs. Bailey ordered. Tyler bit down on his lip. Mrs. Bailey knew that he and Freckle were best friends. She should have chosen him to take the things to the office. He looked over at the Viking who sat staring into space. If Tyler hadn't gotten into trouble with the Vike, Mrs. Bailey would have picked him, Tyler was sure.

"Why do there have to be people like the Viking in the world, anyway?" Tyler mumbled under his breath. Oh, great, now he's looking at me! Tyler lowered his eyes, but he could still hear the Viking's snarl.

"I'll get you, Tidy Wipe."

Snarl was a word they had just had in spelling, and Tyler thought of the Viking the minute he read one of the word's meanings: "To growl angrily or viciously, as a dog."

I wonder if he was born like that, Tyler was thinking. Do babies snarl? His thoughts were suddenly interrupted by Mrs. Bailey.

"Tyler, are you with us? You seem to be having a difficult time concentrating today," she said.

"Uh, I'm listening, really," Tyler stammered.

"Well, good, because I want everyone to pay attention as I explain our new project for history. It's called "People Who Have Shaped Our World." You will all do a two-page written report, as well as an oral presentation," she said. "The bulletin board in the back will be devoted to this project. And everyone will participate in putting it together. I have a cardboard box up on my desk. It's filled with the names of famous figures who have helped shape our world." Mrs. Bailey stopped talking and nodded to Patrick Kessler, who had raised his hand.

"Will there be famous figures, like Garfield?" Patrick asked.

"No, Pat, I'm afraid not." Mrs. Bailey smiled. "These aren't cartoon figures, they're real people: explorers, inventors, world leaders, artists, and thinkers, who have influenced a great many people."

"I know a lot of people who have been influenced by Garfield," Patrick grumbled.

"I also want you to learn how to work together," Mrs. Bailey continued. "So you will be working in pairs." She shook her head as a number of hands shot up. "I will choose the pairs, so when your name is called please come up to my desk. The first pair is Samantha Weiss and Mary Kay." Both girls walked up to the desk. Mrs. Bailey told Samantha to close her eyes and reach into the box.

"Marco Polo," Samantha read aloud from the little paper that she had chosen.

"Drats!" Tyler groaned. He would have loved to have gotten Marco Polo. Everyone was suddenly quiet, waiting to see who the next pair would be and who they would choose as their famous person. Mrs. Bailey continued to call people up. Tyler shifted uneasily in his seat. Who would be his partner? Suddenly his heart sank as he heard Mrs. Bailey call, "Jay Kosa and Becky Zwigler. Hopefully Jay will be back with us tomorrow." Mrs. Bailey offered the box to Becky.

"Amelia Earhart," Becky read the name aloud.

"Should make for an interesting report." Mrs. Bailey smiled.

Poor Freck, Tyler thought. Not only does he have a girl for his partner, but his famous person is a girl too! That's got to be the worst combination. Tyler's eyes locked with Mrs. Bailey's, as she called his name.

"Tyler and . . ." Mrs. Bailey looked around the room. Tyler stiffened. "And Michael." Michael Miller stood up. Tyler felt his shoulders begin to relax, but before they could, Mrs. Bailey motioned for Michael Miller to sit back down. "No, not you, Michael," she said. "I meant Michael Beidelman. Tyler Harrison and Michael Beidelman."

Michael Beidelman! Michael Beidelman! Please, anybody but Michael Beidelman! Tyler sank down into his seat. Meanwhile, his new partner let out a low snarl that developed into a groan.

My feelings exactly, Tyler thought as he dragged himself up to Mrs. Bailey's desk. The girls were giggling and the boys were laughing as he stood next to the Vike. Tyler knew what they were all thinking. Look how funny the giant and the dwarf look standing side by side. Tyler caught a glimpse of Michael Beidelman's face. The Viking looked as embarrassed as he was.

What was Mrs. Bailey thinking of? She knows that we hate each other, Tyler thought as he stood frowning in front of her desk. Mrs. Bailey quieted the class and then held the box out to Tyler. He reached in and pulled out a little slip of paper.

"Leonardo da . . . da . . ." he stammered.

"Da Vinci. Leonardo da Vinci," Mrs. Bailey said. "A famous Renaissance artist. You two should have a good time with this report."

"Way to go, Tidy Wipe. Picked a real winner," the Viking grumbled, as they made their way back to their seats. Tyler sank into his chair and sighed so heavily he blew his paper off his desk.

How could a person's luck be so bad? Tyler reached down to pick up the paper. Of all the partners I could have gotten, I got the snarling Viking, he thought. And of all the famous people I could have gotten, I got some old artist! And to top it all off, a powerful wizard has got my bike.

Tyler's eyes were closed as he sat with his head in his hands. He couldn't stop thinking about old man Quigley. He must certainly be a wizard, but what kind of wizard? Were there such things as good wizards? He tried to imagine the kind-looking old man conjuring up demons and casting evil spells, but he wasn't able to. Quentin Quigley had to be a good wizard. Tyler was sure of it.

Suddenly he cracked one eye open. He had an idea. It had been a bad day, maybe the worst day of his life, but the day wasn't over yet. Tyler knew that all the kids thought he was a wimp, just because of his size, but he would show them. He would show them that he had as much courage as anybody.

By 3:15 the other kids were packing up their backpacks and putting on their coats. Danny Featherman came over and stood beside Tyler's desk.

"Do you want to come over to my house today?" Danny asked. "My grandma is staying with us, and I know where she keeps her wigs.

I can sneak one out of her room and we can fool around with it, if you want to."

Tyler shook his head. Any other time, the offer to fool around with Danny Featherman's grandmother's wig would have seemed inviting, but not today.

"Thanks, but I can't," Tyler told him. "I've got some other stuff to do."

"What stuff?" Danny wanted to know.

Tyler just smiled and shook his head.

By 3:35 the Rainbow Mission was in full swing. The sun had dipped behind a cloud, and the wind was whistling through the trees as Tyler Harrison slowly made his way alone down Dewberry Street.

CHAPTER EIGHT

Tyler stood looking at the old bicycle shop. It seemed as solid and unmovable as all the other buildings along the street. Standing before it now, he found it hard to believe that only yesterday it had actually vanished into thin air. He looked up at the small wooden wheel that hung above the door.

"The wheel of time waits for no man." Tyler read the words aloud again, feeling a shiver of fear run through him. What if old man Quigley did turn boys into frogs or parrots? Tyler bit down on his lip. If I walk into that bicycle shop, I might never walk out again, he thought. I might fly out, or leap out, but never walk again.

He began to think of all the things that he would miss if he were no longer a boy. He wouldn't be able to take a walk to the corner store with his mother, or play football with Lee, or ride bikes with Freckle, or fool around with Danny Featherman and his grandmother's wig. Life would be so empty.

But then Tyler remembered his day in school, and all his feelings of humiliation came rushing back. "I'm not afraid, I'm not afraid," he whispered under his breath. He clutched his flute case with one hand, and turned the old worn doorknob of Quigley's Bicycle Shop with the other.

As Tyler stepped inside, he was overcome with the sound of music, a haunting melody that was coming from the back room. All his fears suddenly fell away as he was wrapped in the graceful magic of the music.

"Company's come, company's come," Verrocchio suddenly cried. Tyler looked up to see the parrot flying out of the back room, the old man behind him.

"Hello, little one." The old man smiled. Ordinarily, Tyler would have hated to be called "little one," but somehow he liked the way Quentin Quigley said it.

"The music . . . it . . . it sounded strange,"

Tyler mumbled. "It didn't sound like any music I've ever heard before. Was it a flute?"

"Ah, yes, my pipe, it's one of my own designs," the old man said. He held up what looked like a recorder to Tyler. It was made of wood, and instead of the usual finger holes, it had long slits that ran down the length of it.

"It sure doesn't look like my flute," Tyler said, shaking his head.

"Your flute? Have you invented an instrument as well?" the old man asked.

"Well, no," Tyler told him, "I never really thought about inventing musical instruments. I guess there are all kinds of things you can invent, when you think about it."

"An amazing amount of things." The old man's lips curled into a smile.

"But if you were a wizard and had magic powers," Tyler said, looking bravely into the old man's eyes, "you wouldn't have to invent things. You could just wish for them."

"That's true. But you don't have to be a wizard to use magic," the old man said.

"You don't?"

"No, nature offers all the magic we need to power our dreams."

Tyler scratched his head. "So are you a wizard or an inventor?" he asked.

The old man laughed. "Definitely not a wizard, I can assure you, though because of my inventions some have called me so."

Tyler let out a sigh of relief. "You must be one great inventor! I want to be a great inventor myself, one day."

"And what would you invent?" the old man wanted to know.

"Right now, I wish I could invent something to make me grow taller," Tyler told him.

The old man shook his head. "Has your small size given you so much heartache?"

Tyler hesitated as he lowered his eyes to the floor. He hadn't talked to anyone, not even Freckle, about this problem, and it was the biggest problem he had.

"It's just that the other kids all make fun of me," Tyler said softly, raising his eyes. "I'm the shortest kid in my class. I guess I take after my father. He's pretty short for a grown-up."

"Have you talked to your father about this?" the old man asked.

"No, he lives across the country with his new wife and their baby. It's weird, I want to take after him, but I just wish it wasn't that part, the short part, you know?"

"Yes, I know what a challenge it is to be different," the old man replied. "I, myself, have spent a lifetime being different."

"You do look strange," Tyler agreed.

"Oh, really?" The old man laughed. "Actually, I was speaking of my mind, not my body."

"Oh, I'm sorry," Tyler said.

"Perfectly understandable." The old man chuckled. "I suppose I am a bit of an old donkey now, although at one time I was quite a handsome fellow. But you see, little one, being handsome is all on the outside. Young or old, handsome or ugly, tall or short, it's what's going on inside that's important. And inside of my handsome head was someone who was always thinking very differently from most people."

"Did you ever try and think like other people, so you wouldn't have to be so different?" Tyler asked.

The old man's eyebrows arched. "Now that is a thought that never entered my head. No, I should imagine the world would be a very boring place if we were all to try and think alike. It would be a waste of the gifts we've been given."

"What kind of gifts?" Tyler wanted to know.

The old man smiled and knocked on Tyler's head with his knuckles. "Your imagination, for one," he said. "It will help you face many a challenge. Now about this flute that you mentioned. I would love to see it and to hear you play. Is it there in the case?"

"Yes," Tyler said, taking off his backpack. He was about to unlock his flute case when Verrocchio swooped down and landed on his shoulder. Tyler's mouth dropped open as he turned his head and found his nose in the parrot's feathers. Tyler had never smelled parrot feathers before, so he took a little sniff. They smelled kind of spicy. He decided to take another sniff. The parrot took offense at all the sniffing, and gently pecked Tyler's nose with his beak.

"Verrocchio," the old man scolded, "what has become of your manners?" Then, turning to Tyler, he added, "You have yet to tell us your name."

"Tyler, uh . . . Tyler Harrison," Tyler yelped as he felt the bird's claws digging into his jacket.

"We would be most honored, Maestro Harrison, if you would grace us with a song." The old man smiled and nodded to the flute case.

Tyler bent down and put the case on the floor, while Verrocchio stuck fast to his shoulder. Carefully, Tyler removed the long silver flute and the old man's eyes lit up.

"I haven't been taking lessons that long," Tyler began to explain, but the old man shook his head, motioning for him to begin to play. Tyler took a deep breath and tried to concentrate. Then he put the flute to his mouth and played "Mississippi Hotcakes" all the way through, without making a single mistake.

"Bravo! Bravo!" The old man nodded and clapped his hands. Tyler grinned and offered the instrument to him.

"So, the flute, this is your flute!" the old man marveled. He ran his fingers over the keys, gently inspecting the instrument. "Yes, it's as I imagined," he whispered. Then he placed the flute to his lips and blew a few

r memory.
hispered.
tudies of
e to the
stand.
d are
k the
ute.
ob-
ns
d

and then as he
. Finally he began
y that was so strange
couldn't believe the
om the same flute on
een playing "Mississippi

ie old man exclaimed. "And
ogether." He handed the flute
and picked up his "pipe." Then
r Tyler to begin. Tyler put his lips
thpiece and began to play "Missis-
cakes" again. (It was the only song
knew all the way through.) With the
paniment of the old man's "pipe," "Mis-
ppi Hotcakes" was transformed into a
vely piece of music. Even Verrocchio lis-
ened quietly.

The old man's eyes twinkled as he came to the end of the piece. Tyler looked up to see the sun's rays pouring in through the big display window. Everything in the shop was suddenly shimmering in the late afternoon light. Neither of them spoke as they savored those first moments after the last notes had been played. The air trembled with thei

"*Magnifico*," the old man finally w
Then he began to chatter away. "My
the tendons were correct in leading n
discovery of the linkage of the keys."

"Tendons? Keys?" Tyler didn't unde

"Yes, the tendons in the human ha
similar to the system of wires that lin
keyboard and the closing pads on your f
You see, the inventor must first be the
server. But alas, all too often my observati
lead me far from my original intent. If I h
had the time . . . Ah, but time itself has cap
tured my imagination. The notion of transcending time is a temptress not easily
resisted. Do you ever think of time, little
one?"

"Time? Like having to wait all the time for
things to happen?" Tyler asked.

The old man laughed. "For the young, there
is too much time, but as one grows older, there
is never enough. I see that that much has not
changed. And yet so very much has, and I
need to find the time to record it all before I
leave."

"Leave?" Tyler mumbled, the smile suddenly leaving his face. "You're not planning on leaving right now, are you?"

"Yes, I've been preparing for my departure for some time. Before I go, though, there is still much to be done." The old man turned and walked behind the counter, where he sat down on a wooden stool. The counter was strewn with papers and leather-bound note-books, so that the cash register was nearly buried. The old man picked up a long pointed pen and dipped it in a little glass bottle of ink. He sat writing for a few minutes, his head bowed over his paper.

"I had no idea that my travels would require me to learn this new language. English has served me well, though the writing has proved somewhat more difficult," the old man said. "I must take my time."

Tyler looked down at the long piece of parchment paper that hung over the counter. He tried to read the writing but couldn't make out the letters. What was Mr. Quigley writing anyway? he wondered. And why was he using that strange pen and ink? Tyler scratched his head.

"It is in code," the old man continued. "An

inventor sometimes needs to keep his discoveries a secret. On reflection, you'd be able to discover the message."

Tyler didn't understand. He looked up to see the old man's forehead wrinkle with worry.

"Ah, but it grows late. Now you do remember your promise, don't you?" the old man whispered. "No one is to know about Quigley's Bicycle Shop. It is most important that you keep this secret."

"Yes, I remember," Tyler told him. "I haven't told anyone."

The old man's face seemed to relax. "Very good," he said. "The bicycle shop is now closing for the day, so we must say good-bye to you, Maestro Harrison. Come, Verrocchio, it is time for your nap." The old man held out his hand. The parrot gave a little squawk, flying from Tyler's shoulder and landing on his master's outstretched fingers.

"Good-bye," Tyler mumbled as he packed up his flute. Then he slipped his backpack on and walked to the door. As he turned the worn doorknob, he stopped, remembering his bicycle. "But what about my chain?" he called, looking back at Quentin Quigley.

"The bicycle chain!" The old man looked up from his writing and laughed. "Some shopkeeper I've turned out to be! Can you come back tomorrow? I promise I'll have given it my attention by then."

Tyler nodded and grinned. He was glad to have another excuse to visit Quigley's Bicycle Shop.

"Oh, and I forgot to ask you about the building and the rainbow," Tyler called excitedly from the door.

The old man winked at the parrot, who was now strutting about on the counter. "One should always make time for a rainbow, eh, Verrocchio?" he whispered. Then he dipped his pen back into the ink bottle, bowed his head, and continued to write.

Once outside, Tyler whistled "Mississippi Hotcakes" as he walked down Dewberry Street. The old man wasn't a wizard at all, he thought, but an inventor. Why didn't we think of that? And he probably wants to keep his shop a secret because he's got some great secret inventions that he's working on, like moving buildings through the air.

Tyler smiled. Playing the flute with Quentin

Quigley was an experience he knew he would never forget. Tyler could hardly wait to tell Freckle about it. And the secret code. Wait until Freck hears about writing in a secret code. Maybe the old man would even teach it to him. Tyler jumped over a crack in the sidewalk.

This day started out being the worst one of my life, Tyler thought. And ended up being the best! He remembered how frightened he'd been, frightened that Quentin Quigley was a wizard who would turn him into a parrot or a frog. Tyler looked at his legs and laughed.

"And I'm walking!" he shouted. "I'm a boy and I'm walking!" He kept his head down, watching his legs in motion as he continued along the street. And that's when Tyler Harrison the boy walked straight into Michael Beidelman the Viking!

CHAPTER NINE

"Agh!" Tyler screamed, dropping his flute case on the Viking's foot!

"Ow!" the Viking wailed. Then, when he'd recovered, he asked, "Where have you been?"

Tyler gritted his teeth. "I was just walking," he said.

"I saw you come out of that bike shop." The Viking sneered. "Come to think of it . . ." He cocked his head and looked down the street. "I don't remember a bike shop ever being there before."

"Well, it . . . it . . . just opened," Tyler stammered. "Actually they haven't really had their grand opening and they don't want anyone to know about it yet."

"Why not?"

"Be . . . be . . . because they want it to be a surprise," Tyler said nervously.

"Something's not right about this," the Viking growled. "Just what are you trying to hide, anyway, Tidy Wipe?"

Tyler stood biting his lip. Michael Beidelman, his worst enemy, knew his best secret! If the Viking wanted to, he could tell every kid in school about the bike shop. Quentin Quigley's secret was in grave danger of becoming common knowledge. Tyler realized that drastic measures were called for.

"Vike, how would you like to join our secret club?" he blurted out. "If you keep the bike shop a secret, you can become a member."

"I don't know," the Viking hesitated. "Who else is in the club, anyway?"

"Just Freckle and me," Tyler told him. "We're the only ones who know about the bike shop. It's a secret club."

"Why don't you want anyone else to know about it?"

"Because then it wouldn't be a secret anymore," Tyler explained. "Just think, we're the only kids in the whole school who know this secret. And if you keep the secret, you can come to the first meeting in our clubhouse tomorrow after school."

The Viking stood, thinking it over. "OK, but if this club turns out to be stupid," he said, "I'm going to tell everyone about it and about the bike shop too."

That night Tyler called Freckle on the phone. Mrs. Kosa answered, and told Tyler that Freckle wasn't feeling well and had gone to bed.

The next morning, when the Harrisons' phone rang at 6:00 A.M., Tyler's mother answered it in her room.

"Tyler, my alarm clock hasn't gone off yet and you're getting phone calls already," she called out groggily. Tyler stumbled out of bed and dragged himself to the kitchen phone. It was Freckle. He had fallen asleep at 6:00 P.M. the day before and had slept straight through the night. His fever was gone and his throat felt better. Freckle was known for his miraculous recoveries. He claimed that his freckles were responsible. Tyler could hear the burst of energy in his friend's voice.

"I'm glad you're feeling OK, because I've got some good news and some bad news," Tyler croaked.

"Wait, Ty, you've got to hear this," Freckle interrupted.

Tyler listened as a series of squeaks came over the line.

"Isn't that great?" Freckle asked after the last squeak.

"Great," Tyler groaned. "What was it?"

"Wrinkles!" Freckle exclaimed. "That was Wrinkles saying good morning!" Wrinkles was Freckle's pet hamster. "I just taught him to do that, isn't it great? So what were you saying? Something about good and bad news?"

"Yeah, which do you want first?" Tyler asked.

"Give me the good," Freckle said.

"The good news is that Quentin Quigley is not a wizard," Tyler whispered into the phone.

"But the building," Freckle interrupted. "We saw the building in the air."

"What we saw was one of the old man's inventions," Tyler told him. "He's an inventor, not a wizard."

"Are you sure?"

"Pretty sure."

"So what's the bad news?" Freckle wanted to know. There was a long silence at the other end.

"We had a new member join our club yesterday," Tyler finally said in a little voice.

"I thought you said it was a secret club and no one else could join," Freckle objected.

"I had to make an exception," Tyler tried to explain.

"Don't tell me," Freckle interrupted. "Danny Featherman."

"No, not Danny."

"Marc Freer?"

"No, not Marc, Michael." Tyler winced as he said it.

"Michael Miller?" Freckle asked.

"No, the other Michael," Tyler whispered. "Michael Beidelman."

"Michael Beidelman!" Freckle yelled. "Not Mike the Vike! Not the Viking! Not *that* Michael Beidelman!" he wailed.

CHAPTER TEN

It took Tyler a long time to explain all that had happened. Freckle's wails finally subsided to grumbles, and he even stopped grumbling altogether when Tyler mentioned that he might be learning a secret code soon. The boys went ahead and planned the first meeting for after school in Freckle's clubhouse. They decided that like it or not they would have to be nice to the Viking, now that he had joined their club.

The next morning on their way to school, Tyler looked warily up the street, to see the Viking walking with the usual group of second and third graders. Freckle knelt down and opened his lunch box on the sidewalk. The two friends always opened their lunch boxes after they had turned the corner near Freckle's house. Trading food was an important part of their day.

"So what do you have to trade?" Freckle wanted to know. "Any potato chips?" Freckle loved potato chips, but since his mother had stopped buying all "junk food," they were off her shopping list. "You are so lucky." He sighed as he watched Tyler pull a small bag of chips out of his lunch box.

Tyler's mother loved potato chips and he often had little bags packed in his lunch. However, she refused to buy cupcakes, so he would save his chips to trade with Marc, whose mother always packed cupcakes.

"Have you got any of that kiwi stuff?" Tyler asked, looking in Freckle's open box. Tyler liked kiwis almost as much as cupcakes. He traded half a bag of potato chips for three kiwi slices wrapped in plastic wrap. He put the slices in his lunch box and poured the chips into Freckle's hand.

Freckle could never wait until lunch to eat the forbidden food, so he would stuff the goodies in the pocket of his jeans. That way he could sample them whenever he wanted to.

The boys closed their lunch boxes and continued down the street.

When they finally walked into their classroom, they found Mrs. Bailey on her way out.

"I've got to run over and borrow a map from Mr. Gazo's room," she announced. "I'll only be a few minutes." She hurried out the door. Tyler and Freckle walked to the back closet and hung up their coats, then joined Danny and Theo who were fooling around with Fido, the class rabbit. They took their seats and watched Marc Freer and Max Silvestri, who were up at the board drawing funny-looking space aliens and writing girls' names under them.

Freckle reached into his pocket and grabbed a handful of crumbled potato chips. He quickly shoved some into his mouth. He had mastered the technique of chewing potato chips in class without making a sound. It involved a steady eye and a fine-tuned ear, watching Mrs. Bailey closely and chewing during the noisiest times. Freckle was enjoying the luxury of crunching away noisily, since Mrs. Bailey had left the room. He reached into his pocket and pulled out another handful of chips.

"Ugh!" he suddenly cried, looking down at his hand. "I forgot that I put some hamster food in my pocket this morning for Wrinkles, and it got kind of mixed up with the potato chips. I almost ate hamster food!" He sat looking down at the chips and nuggets in his hand, then began to smile. "Hey, Ty, what do you think? Maybe I just invented a new snack food. I could call it Wrinkle Chips!"

"Great," Tyler said, shaking his head. "And maybe after you eat it, you'll be able to squeak good morning, just like Wrinkles."

"I wonder what it tastes like?" Freckle mused.

"Trust me, Freck, no matter what it tastes like, I don't know anybody who would want to eat hamster food. Do you?"

"Well, besides Wrinkles, no, I can't think of anybody," Freckle said, picking a chip out of his hand. "But people eat all kinds of weird things. I bet there is somebody who would eat this."

"So when's the meeting of this stupid club?" a loud voice suddenly boomed behind them. Tyler stiffened and turned around. The Viking was walking toward them.

"Have you told anyone about the secret?" Tyler asked anxiously.

"Not yet," the Viking told him. "Hey, Freckle, what are you eating?" Ordinarily Freckle's snacks would have been off bounds to the Viking, but now that the Viking had something over them, he was determined to take advantage of the situation. "Looks good," the Viking said, holding out his hand. "What's it called?"

Freckle shook his head. "Gee, Vike, I don't think you want to eat this. It's really not . . ."

The Viking grinned. "Give me all of it," he ordered. "I want all of it. What did you say it's called?"

"Wrinkle Chips," Freckle told him, emptying the little brown nuggets and chips into the Viking's hand. "They're called Wrinkle Chips."

CHAPTER ELEVEN

Tyler and Freckle kept a close eye on the Viking all through math. When he burped loudly during reading, Freckle almost fell off his chair laughing. Tyler looked over to see the Viking making a face as the Wrinkle Chips left a distinct aftertaste in his mouth.

"I think I'll bring some lettuce in for him tomorrow," Freckle whispered to Tyler. "That way the fur on his stomach will stay nice and shiny." The two traded hamster jokes all morning, until Mrs. Bailey made an announcement.

"All right, class, it's time to break into your pairs for our history projects," she said. "We'll go to the library, where you'll find the books you'll need for your research. Tomorrow's assignment is an outline that lists the important dates in your famous figure's life. You can divide the work, and there should be enough books for each of you to take home, in case you haven't finished in class. Please line up with your partner."

Tyler waited for the very last moment before leaving his desk and standing beside the Viking. Everyone slowly filed out of the classroom, walking in pairs down the hall. As Tyler walked beside his hulking partner, he remembered what Mr. Quigley had said about his imagination. "It will help you face many a challenge."

Tyler stole a glance at Michael Beidelman and imagined what it would be like to have such a big, powerful body. Then he imagined himself even bigger than the Viking, bigger than all the kids in his class, bigger than Mrs. Bailey. He looked up to the ceiling in the hallway and thought about what it would be like to have his head grazing it. He didn't see how all this imagining was going to help him, but it did make the time go by.

Once the fifth graders had reached the library and taken their turns at the card catalog, they went off in search of their books. Tyler walked down the biography aisle with the Viking close behind.

"Let see, J . . . K . . . L. There are the Ls," the Viking said, pointing to a shelf above Tyler's head. They stood scanning the shelf until they came to the books on Leonardo.

"Here he is," Tyler said, reaching for a number of books. He read their titles aloud. *"Leonardo da Vinci: The Man Who Wanted to Know Everything; Leonardo da Vinci: Genius of the Renaissance; The Master Leonardo.* This should be enough," he said, handing the books to Michael Beidelman. The Viking grunted and carried them over to a table.

"Danny and Theo get to do their report on the Wright Brothers. Marc and Tony get Neal Armstrong. And look who we get stuck with," the Viking muttered. "This is going to be the most boring report, and it's all your fault," he said, sitting down.

"We weren't allowed to see who we were picking," Tyler reminded him as he sank into a chair. "I hate getting stuck with this old guy just as much as you do, believe me," he said.

(But he was really thinking, just as much as I hate getting stuck with you.)

"So let's see if we can finish this outline before the period ends. There must be something interesting in here that we can use," Tyler mumbled as he began to page through one of the books. " 'Leonardo da Vinci of Italy—1452–1519,' " he read aloud. " 'Leonardo was a painter, writer, musician, inventor, and scientist.' Gee, he did a lot of different stuff," Tyler said as he copied the dates into his notebook.

" 'The Renaissance was the rebirth of man out of the dark years of medieval superstition and belief. It was a return to the light of human reason. From the Renaissance to the twentieth century, the work of Leonardo transcends time.' Transcends time . . . " Tyler whispered the words again. Where had he heard that phrase?

He turned the page and came to a chapter titled "The Painter." Tyler looked over the pictures of saints and angels until he came to one he recognized. "Look, he painted the Mona Lisa," Tyler said, holding the book up for the Viking to see.

"Big deal." The Viking yawned. Tyler continued to turn the pages until he came to some drawings of horses and soldiers.

"Now, that's pretty cool," the Viking whispered as he pointed to a picture of a battle. Both boys peered down at the amazing battle scenes depicted before them. They were drawn with all the fury and force of real live horses and men charging in war. The men's faces were anguished and pained as they fell wounded to the ground.

Tyler slowly turned the pages until they came to the chapter titled: "Il Cavallo: The Horse." The Viking moved closer as Tyler began to read aloud. " 'In the evening, May 17, 1491. Here a record shall be kept of everything related to the bronze horse presently under execution.' "

As Tyler turned the pages, the Viking kept leaning closer, until he was almost on top of the book.

"I love horses," he mumbled, poring over the detailed drawings.

"You do?" Tyler asked. He had never imagined that the Viking loved anything.

"When we lived in Indiana, I had a horse.

His name was String Bean," the Viking told him.

"String Bean?" Tyler began to laugh and the Viking grinned. Tyler sat looking at his partner as if he were seeing him for the first time. When he wasn't scowling, the Viking looked almost nice, Tyler decided. He had never noticed how blue the Viking's eyes were, or the way he tilted his head to one side when he grinned. As he listened to the Viking's laughter, Tyler began to feel bad about letting him eat the Wrinkle Chips. Suddenly Mrs. Woodring, the librarian, was standing before them.

"I realize you have to discuss your report, but please do it quietly," she said in her soft, velvety library voice.

Tyler resumed their discussion in a hushed whisper. "Why did you name him String Bean?"

"Because he was the skinniest horse you ever saw," the Viking told him. "Just like a string bean. My dad said that he was the cheapest horse around, because he looked so bad. I named him String Bean, but I promised him that I would change his name to Charger just as soon as I fattened him up."

"Did you fatten him up?" Tyler wanted to know.

"I did, but it took a long time. After about a year, he looked great, but by then I was so used to calling him String Bean, I couldn't start calling him Charger."

"Where is he now?" Tyler asked.

"I had to leave him in Indiana when we moved." The Viking frowned and looked away.

"It must have been hard to leave String Bean behind," Tyler whispered. The Viking didn't say anything. Both boys shifted in their seats uneasily as they suddenly realized that they were having a friendly conversation, one that didn't include insults and threats. That was another thing that Tyler had never imagined. There was an uncomfortable silence, then both boys quickly returned to Leonardo da Vinci.

" 'Leonardo and Music,' " Tyler began reading a new chapter aloud. " 'Leonardo was a great performer and teacher of music. He invented a considerable number of ingenious musical instruments and made improvements on existing ones.' "

Tyler turned the page and his mouth

dropped open at the sight of a flute with a drawing of a hand above it. " 'These drawings from Leonardo's anatomy notebooks illustrate how he may have been inspired to solve the problem of opening and closing the holes of wind instruments. He found the analogy for a system of wires with which he could link the keyboard and the closing pads in the tendons of the hand.' "

"So turn the page, already," the Viking demanded. "Who cares about some old flute."

"It's what Mr. Quigley told me," said Tyler.

"Who's Mr. Quigley?" the Viking asked. Tyler hesitated a moment as he remembered his promise to the old man. Then he thought about the Viking's joining the club and decided that since he already knew about the shop, knowing a little more couldn't hurt.

"Quentin Quigley is the old man who has the bike shop on Dewberry Street," Tyler answered. "When I was in there yesterday, he told me all about the tendons in the hand being like the keyboard of a flute. And look, do you see that recorder?" Tyler pointed to a picture of a recorder with long slits running down the side of it, instead of the usual finger holes.

"Mr. Quigley made a recorder just like that. He played it for me."

"So, what's the big deal?" The Viking shrugged. "He probably read the book. Maybe he knows a lot about Leonardo da Vinci, and he made the recorder after seeing it in the book."

"No, you don't understand." Tyler tried to explain. "He didn't just make the instrument. He said that he invented it."

"So he lied," the Viking suggested. But Tyler sat shaking his head. Quentin Quigley did not seem like the kind of man who would lie, but what other explanation could there be?

CHAPTER TWELVE

"Save me from Becky Banana Breath," Freckle moaned, coming up to Tyler's table. "She told me that she eats four bananas a day. I think she must be part monkey. So how's your report coming?" He sat down beside Tyler, without looking up at the Viking.

"Uh, . . . it's interesting," Tyler mumbled, his head still bent over the book.

"Interesting? Some old artist is interesting?" Freckle looked skeptical.

"He wasn't just an artist, Freck," Tyler said, looking up. "He was an inventor too. He invented musical instruments, just like Mr. Quigley."

"Was he also a wizard?" Freckle smirked.

"A wizard?" The Viking's eyebrows shot up.

"Oh, Freckle thought that Mr. Quigley was

a wizard," Tyler said. "He can do some amazing things, like making buildings rise up in the air without a crane or anything. And just think, if this was the book he learned to make the flute from, he could have learned all kinds of other things from it."

"Please make sure that you've all checked out your books," Mrs. Bailey announced. "And remember, tomorrow I'll be expecting your finished outlines." Tyler looked down at his notebook. He had only written two dates at the top of his page.

"Come on, Vike," he said, gathering up the books, "I'll check this one out. And you can take that one. We'll just divide his life in half. We can figure it out later when we meet in the clubhouse."

"Where is this clubhouse, anyway?" the Viking wanted to know.

Tyler looked around to be sure that no one else was listening. "It's in the old red shed behind Freckle's house," he whispered. "Don't forget, you promised not to tell anyone." The Viking suddenly resumed his bully pose. It was as if their earlier conversation about String Bean had never taken place. The

Viking puckered his lips, and his eyes narrowed to two little mean slits.

"I'll think about it," the Viking snarled. "This club sounds kind of stupid. I might have some better stuff to do today."

"Oh, great," Tyler sighed as he watched the Viking walk away. "What if he doesn't want to come? What if he decides to tell everyone about the bike shop?"

"Don't worry," said Freckle, "he doesn't have anything better to do. He'll come."

That afternoon, Tyler and Freckle hurried down Market Street on their way home from school. They wanted to get to their clubhouse as fast as they could.

Tyler was busy spreading out a blanket on the floor of Freckle's shed when he heard footsteps outside. "Now, remember, Freck," Tyler whispered, "we've got to be nice to the Viking as long as he's in the club."

Freckle made a face. "That won't be easy," he said in a low voice.

"What a stupid-looking clubhouse," the Viking grumbled as he walked into the shed.

"Why, you . . . " Freckle's face reddened under his freckles.

"Why, you made it, Vike," Tyler yelled, jumping up. "We're really glad you could come."

"Yeah, so now what?" the Viking asked, looking around with a yawn. Tyler tapped his fingers on the blanket. He hadn't figured out just what the club would be doing yet.

"Well, we could tell some ghost stories," he suggested.

"Ghost stories? Is that all you do in this club?" The Viking smirked. "Ghost stories, that's it?"

Freckle looked over at Tyler as if to say, he's right, this does seem like a boring thing for a club to be doing.

"Well, no," Tyler hesitated, trying to think of something to say. "We have a lot of different club business to . . ." He was suddenly interrupted by a loud bang on the shed roof. This was followed by a chorus of giggles and another loud bang. The three boys jumped, and Freckle carefully cracked open the door.

"Oh, no," he whispered, "we're under attack!"

"From who?" Tyler wanted to know.

"It looks like Tony and Kevin and some

other little kids," Freckle said. "They've got a bucket of black walnuts with them. Tony has a black walnut tree in his yard. I wonder how they found out about our meeting?" Both he and Tyler turned and looked suspiciously at the Viking. Tyler held his hands over his ears as another volley of walnuts crashed onto the shed's tin roof.

"We should have known better than to trust you with our club's secrets," Freckle said to the Vike.

"Oh, yeah?" the Viking sneered. "For your information, I had nothing to do with this attack. Tony probably saw you come in here from his yard."

"We're supposed to believe that?" Freckle muttered.

"Are you calling me a liar?" The Viking's face had gone completely red.

"Nobody is calling anybody a liar," Tyler said firmly. "Just hold on and we can sort this all out."

"Sorry, Tidy Wipe, but I have better things to do than fool around with you two. I've just decided to start a club of my own and for our first club business, I'm going to tell all my

members about that dinky old bike shop and that weird old man. By tomorrow, the whole school will know about it." The Viking smiled broadly, displaying his big white teeth, as another nut crashed against the shed.

CHAPTER THIRTEEN

"Hold your fire!" the Viking yelled, running from the shed into Tony's yard. Tyler and Freckle quickly shut the door as another wave of nuts crashed against the roof.

They sat with their backs to the door, waiting for the assault to end. Tyler's black hair fell over his eyes as he lowered his head in his hands.

"Maybe we shouldn't have accused the Vike," Tyler said. "We really don't know if he did tell Tony and the others."

"It doesn't make any difference now," Freckle sighed. "By tomorrow the whole school will know about the bike shop."

"I blew it," Tyler said hoarsely. "I trusted the Vike with Mr. Quigley's secret and now he's going to tell everyone."

"It's not your fault, Ty." Freckle tried to console him. "He was walking down Dewberry Street and saw the shop all by himself. You didn't point it out to him."

"I might as well have," Tyler groaned. "If I hadn't called him the Worm on Wormwood Avenue, he probably wouldn't have followed me home. It's all my fault." The two friends waited until the enemy had used up all its ammunition. Then they stepped outside the shed.

"I've got to warn Mr. Quigley," Tyler said as they crossed Freckle's yard.

"What do you mean?" Freckle asked.

"I have to tell him that the Vike knows about the shop and is going to tell everyone."

"Not now," Freckle gasped. "You don't mean that you're going now. It's late. Your mom will want you home, and the bike shop will probably be closed."

"My mom has a class tonight and Lee won't care if I come in a little late," Tyler said. "I've just got to try and warn Mr. Quigley. Why don't you come with me?"

Both boys looked up suddenly as they heard Mrs. Kosa calling from the kitchen door.

"Freckle, it's time to come in for supper now."
Freckle waved to her and then looked back at
his friend, his face full of worry.

"I can't come with you," he said. "Not now,
anyway. And you shouldn't go back alone. Just
wait until tomorrow. I'll go with you then."

"Tomorrow may be too late," Tyler called
over his shoulder as he ran out of the yard. He
turned to look back at Freckle, who stood shaking his head, then ran the rest of the way to
Dewberry Street.

When Tyler finally reached Quigley's Bicycle Shop, he pushed the door open and rushed
inside. The lamps on the walls were lit, and
the bicycles gleamed in the flickering light,
but the old man and the parrot were nowhere
to be seen. An uneasy feeling crept over Tyler
as he looked around the store.

Why is it so quiet? he wondered. Where are
Verrocchio and Mr. Quigley? If the shop were
closed, why hadn't the old man locked the
door?

"Mr. Quigley, are you here?" Tyler called.
He moved slowly among the bicycles, making
his way to the back of the store. When he
bumped into a blue tricycle, the bell on the

handlebar rang so loudly that it echoed. Tyler stood listening for the rustle of wings or the sound of footsteps, but all that he could hear was the racing of his own heart.

He cautiously stepped around some more bicycles, until he reached the doorway leading to the back room. A heavy curtain of deep red velvet material hung down in front of it.

"Mr. Quigley," Tyler called, "it's me, Tyler Harrison. Are you back there?" He waited, but there was no reply.

Mr. Quigley must have gone out, Tyler thought as he stood before the curtain. But when would he be coming back? he wondered.

"I'll have to leave him a note," Tyler said under his breath. He climbed up on the old stool at the counter and began to rummage through the pile of papers that was strewn over the countertop. Holding up a long sheet of parchment paper, Tyler tried to read the strange wavy letters. It was written, along with all the other papers on the counter, in the same script as Mr. Quigley's secret code. Did the old man always write like this? he wondered. And if so, why?

Tyler put the paper down and picked up the

long quill pen that was lying beside the ink bottle. He thought about using it, but worried that the ink might splatter over everything. He reached around to his backpack and unzipped one of the pockets. He pulled out a pencil and began searching for a blank sheet of paper on the counter. After finding one, he sat thinking for a few seconds and then started to write.

Dear mr. Quigley,
Someone found out about your shop
and is going to tell the whole
School tomorrow. I am sorry.
Your friend,
     Tyler Harrison

Tyler reached in his pocket and pulled out a sheet of hologram stickers that he had been saving. He pulled off one of the stickers and carefully placed it beside his name. Then he put the note on the cash register so that the old man would be sure to see it.

"Now where did I put the sheet of stickers I just had?" Tyler muttered. He rummaged around on the counter, searching through the stacks of papers. His index finger got stuck in something under a pile of paper. He pulled his hand out of the pile and looked down to see a human skull. Tyler let out a cry as he pulled his finger out of an eye socket!

"Agh!" he gasped, falling backward off the stool. He closed his eyes for a second and saw an image of the old man in his long flowing robe with his silver hair and beard. Whoever heard of an inventor looking like that? "Maybe Freckle was right," Tyler gasped, opening his eyes. "Maybe old man Quigley really is a wizard!"

CHAPTER FOURTEEN

Tyler picked himself up from the floor. "Agh!" he cried again, as he heard a noise behind him. He spun around. A little mouse was scampering across the floor. Tyler breathed a sigh of relief, then stiffened at the thought of the old man returning and finding him there. Whether Quentin Quigley was a wizard or not, Tyler was frightened.

He ran toward the door, bumping into a unicycle and tripping over a wagon attached to a tricycle. By the time Tyler got out of the store, he was shaking all over. He took off down Dewberry Street as fast as he could. He ran until he was exhausted. The sun was setting, and lights were coming on in the houses along the street.

Within minutes, Tyler could see the light on

his own front porch. He smiled and ran toward it. But when he saw his mother's car sitting in the driveway, he groaned and ducked behind the garage.

If he told his mother about the wizard and the skull, she'd know he had gone back to Dewberry Street on his own. It was bad enough that he was out this late. One of the house rules was that he had to be home by five o'clock. Another rule was that he was not to bike past Howel Street alone after dark. Tyler knew that it must be at least six-thirty by now. He also knew that if his mother found out where he had been, she'd probably ground him for life.

I can't lie to her. If she asks me where I've been, I'll have to tell the truth. Tyler bit his lip, contemplating the worst that could happen. His mother would greet him at the door with her, "What am I going to do with you?" face. She had an entire repertoire of looks that expressed her unhappiness. The "What am I going to do with you?" one was the worst (not that he liked any of them). It was the most sour-looking of all her expressions and was always followed with a long speech on the hardships of "being a single parent." It inevitably started with "What am I going to do with you?" and ended with "You're to have no TV, no allowance, and you're grounded until further notice."

Tyler kicked the garbage can. Why did the worst always have to happen? Maybe just this once, the best would happen. Maybe his mother would be in such a good mood that she wouldn't even notice what time it was. Maybe she had gotten a raise or won the lottery. Tyler decided to try and think of what it would be like if the "best" did happen. "What a wonderful son you are, Ty," he could hear his mother coo, a serene smile lighting up her face. "I'm so happy to see you. Sit down, watch some TV, and have a Twinkie." That's more like it, Tyler thought happily.

He kicked the garbage can once more for good luck and walked out from behind the garage. When he reached the porch, his mother opened the door, took one look at him, and said, "What am I going to do with you? Lee and I have been waiting an hour for you to get home." She started putting on her coat. "Lee called me at work, complaining of a sore throat. I skipped my evening class and rushed home to take him to the doctor. But I didn't want to leave until you got home."

She was so anxious to get Lee to the doctor, she didn't even ask Tyler where he'd been. "Lock the door, then eat the supper I put out for you on the kitchen table. After that you're to go straight to your room and do your homework. And don't you dare come down for anything," was all she said.

"What if the phone rings?" Tyler wanted to know.

"Tyler Harrison, I have no time for this." His mother groaned. "Your brother may have a strep throat for all I know. You can answer the phone if it rings, but you are not to call anyone. Now eat your supper and go upstairs."

Tyler stole a glance at Lee, who made a face at him as he walked past him. "He doesn't look sick to me," Tyler grumbled. He locked the door after they left and then walked into the kitchen. He gobbled up his supper, all the while keeping an eye on the phone on the wall by the refrigerator.

Come on, Freck, Tyler was thinking, give your best friend a call. Just pick up the phone and call me. He sat waiting for the phone to ring. If he doesn't call me tonight, Tyler decided impatiently, I'll have to wait until tomorrow morning to tell him about the skull. How can I keep such a secret for so long? Even criminals in jail get to make one phone call.

CHAPTER FIFTEEN

Tyler gave the phone one last look and then dragged his backpack up the stairs to his room. He took off his clothes, changed into his pajamas, and stretched out on the bed, his hands behind his head.

Mr. Quigley, who are you, really? Tyler wondered, closing his eyes. An inventor or a wizard? It's as if you're from another place or time. Tyler's eyes opened suddenly, as he remembered the phrase, "transcends time." He had read it in the book on Leonardo da Vinci, but where else had he heard it?

"Mr. Quigley," Tyler said softly. "He was talking about transcending time too." What did it mean? Tyler got out of bed and walked over to his desk, picking up his dictionary. It

took him a few minutes to find the word "transcend." Tyler read the meaning aloud.

" 'Transcend: One. to go or be above or beyond.' So what does 'transcend time' mean?"
He tried putting the words together. To go to
time, to go above time, to go beyond time. To
go beyond time, but how could a person go
beyond time? Unless that person was a great
inventor or a great wizard?

Tyler jumped at the sound of the phone
ringing. He ran downstairs to the kitchen. It
was Freckle calling to see how he had made
out at the bike shop. Tyler was so excited that
he didn't know where to begin. When he had
finally calmed down, he began talking fast, and
Freckle had to stop him several times, telling
him to "slow down."

"So what you're telling me is that the old
man really could be a wizard and you saw
skulls and stuff in his shop," Freckle whispered.

"Freck, I not only saw a skull, I felt it,"
Tyler said with a wince. They talked for a long
time about wizards and skulls and transcending time.

"I say the old man's a wizard," Freckle concluded. "A real live wizard on Dewberry Street. It's too bad we can't develop some of his powers, and transcend time to jump past tomorrow's homework."

"Homework," Tyler groaned. "I forgot all about it." He quickly hung up the receiver and hurried back to his room. He reached for his backpack, pulling out his notes and the book on Leonardo da Vinci.

Tyler thought about the outline. Was I supposed to work on the first half of his life or the second? He had completely forgotten to talk to Vike about it. So much had happened since the morning, his mind was reeling.

I can't call the Vike, Tyler thought. I'd rather die than call him, besides Mom said no phone calls. I'll just have to do the whole thing, he decided wearily.

Tyler sank down on the bed and began paging through the library book, coming to a chapter titled: "The Great Man's Studio." He read about the ingenious mechanisms that Leonardo da Vinci invented to lower and raise his canvases as he worked on them. He also read about the circular window Leonardo designed. It too was fitted with ropes and pulleys, allowing the artist to raise and lower the window at will.

The book was much too long for Tyler to finish reading in one night, so he paged through the rest of it, copying down important dates in the artist's life.

When he heard the key in the lock downstairs, Tyler jumped off his bed and poked his head out the door. He sighed with relief as he heard Lee and his mother walk into the living room. He ran back to bed and sat looking at his book, listening to their footsteps on the stairs.

"Did you eat all of your supper, hon?" Tyler's mother asked, coming into his room. Tyler smiled, looking up from his book. If she was calling him "hon," it was a sure sign that her mood had improved.

"What did the doctor say about Lee?" he asked as his mother sank down on the bed beside him.

"He took a throat culture," his mother replied, "but he didn't think it looked too bad. There seems to be a bug going around. If Lee takes his medicine and stays in bed for a few days, he should be back on his feet. Speaking of feet, mine are beat." His mother sighed.

Tyler looked up at her tired face. She had dark blue circles under her eyes and her lipstick was all worn off.

"Was it busy at work today, Mom?" he asked.

"Oh, yes, it's payroll day and that's the busiest day of the week," his mother said, kicking off her shoes. "You know, Ty, now that I'm going back to school at nights, there's a good chance I can get a better job. We'll be able to get some things for the house and maybe even a new car someday."

"One with an air bag?" Tyler wanted to know.

His mother smiled. "We'll see. But taking an extra class won't be easy for me, because I'll have to leave you and Lee home alone two nights a week. I need to know that you'll be all right, so I won't be sitting in class worrying. You can't be breaking the house rules like you did tonight."

Tyler shifted uneasily against his pillow. What if she asked him where he'd been? He looked down at his opened book.

"I know that you like to play at Freckle's house, and you can, but you must come home

by four-thirty. I tried calling you ther
but the line was busy every time I
think Freckle's sister Annie lives
phone."

Thank you, Annie, Tyler thought
lief. He looked at his mother. "I w
again, Mom, really I won't." His
smiled and reached over to kiss his
was then that she noticed his book.

"What's all this?" she asked, leanii
get a better look.

"It's for a report I'm doing in histc
about the life of Leonardo da Vinci,"
her.

"Oh, that's great. He was an amaz
His mother picked up the book.

"You know about Leonardo da Vii
asked, surprised.

"Sure I do. You know how I love
I've taken out every art book our l
Don't you remember a few years
I was such a devotee of the arti
O'Keeffe?"

"What's a devotee?" Tyler wante

"It's someone who is devoted to
something. I loved Georgia O'Kee

CHAPTER SI

"Yes," his mother replied, p
book. "They must mention
here. Let me see. Oh, yes.
began to read aloud. " 'Leon
a prolific writer, keeping not
his many observations, ske
He always printed with his le
of the entries in his noteboo
Fearful that his ideas would
fell into the wrong hands, he
terious backwards writing tl
deciphered in the reflection

Tyler's mother put down
nardo da Vinci, what an inc
he must have been," she saic
back on the pillow. She be
other "characters" of the art

read about, but Tyler had stopped listening. He was too busy trying to remember what Mr. Quigley had told him about his secret code.

"It's in code," the old man had whispered. "An inventor sometimes needs to keep his discoveries a secret. On reflection, you'd be able to discover the message."

"Reflection," Tyler mumbled under his breath, looking at the mirror over his dresser. "So that's what he meant by reflection! Mom, do you think there could be any devotees of Leonardo da Vinci? People that might try writing in his secret code?"

"Um, I suppose there are," his mother muttered, looking down at her watch. "But here we go, breaking another house rule." She sighed. "It's after nine and your light should have been out ten minutes ago." She reached over and gave him a kiss.

"Good night, hon," she called, switching off the light and walking to the door.

"Good night," Tyler replied, pulling the blankets over his head. Was Quentin Quigley using the same secret code as Leonardo da

Vinci? Could a wizard be a devotee? And could
there be such a thing as a good wizard?

Tyler poked his head out of his blankets,
turning to face the window. He could see a big
sad-faced moon hanging in the sky above the
old apple tree across the street. The stars were
twinkling brightly as they peeked out from behind the swirls of a long wispy cloud. Tyler lay
staring at a little flurry of stars that hung just
below the moon.

"There's so much that I don't know," he said
to himself. "How am I ever going to figure it
all out?" As he looked up at the sky, he thought
about the rainbow and the beautiful music Mr.
Quigley had played for him.

"I am going back tomorrow," he whispered,
"and I'm not going to run away. I'm going back
into Quigley's Bicycle Shop and I'm going to
get my bike."

The next morning Tyler stood knocking impatiently on Freckle Kosa's front door. He
sighed with relief when the door opened and
Freckle's head of blond curls appeared.

"What are you doing here so early?" Freckle
asked, lifting his pajama shirt and scratching
his stomach.

"I tried calling, but your line was busy," Tyler explained.

"Annie wakes up with the phone to her ear," Freckle said, with a yawn. "My dad says that her ear is going to fall off if she . . ."

"Freck, will you forget about Annie's ear," Tyler interrupted. "Can you leave for school a little early today?"

"Sure," Freckle said. "Do you want to fool around on the playground?"

"No, we won't have time for that," Tyler told him. "We've got some club business to see to, important club business. So can you hurry up?"

"OK, but Wrinkles and I are still in our pajamas. Just hold on while we change." Freckle turned around and ran up the stairs to his room.

"Wrinkles is still in his pajamas?" Tyler wondered aloud, stepping through the doorway. What kind of pajamas does a hamster wear, anyway? He sat down on the bottom step to wait. Wrinkles was the only hamster that Tyler knew who wore pajamas and watched television. Freckle had insisted on treating him more like a brother than a pet.

Since Freckle had been the only boy in a family of two girls, he had always longed for a brother. When his mother came home from the hospital with his little sister Shelly, Freckle was so disappointed that his father ran out and bought him a hamster. It wasn't as good as a brother, but Freckle thought that Wrinkles was a lot cuter than his new red-faced sibling.

Tyler looked up and saw his friend racing down the stairs.

"I've got to tell my mom that I'm leaving," Freckle yelled over his shoulder as he ducked into the kitchen.

"And please make sure that Wrinkles is back in his cage before you go. I don't want to find him asleep in my sneaker again," Tyler heard Mrs. Kosa call as Freckle bounded back into the hall.

"In her sneaker?" Tyler whispered, walking to the door.

"Oh, that was a close call," Freckle giggled, strapping on his backpack. "It's a good thing Wrinkles has such a long tail. My mom was about to put her foot in her sneaker when she saw Wrinkles's tail sticking out. He had crawled way up in the toe. He likes to sleep in cozy, smelly places." Tyler made a face as Freckle turned and looked behind him. "Now where did I put him?"

"Freck, he's in your pocket." Tyler pointed to the tiny black eyes and little pink nose that were sticking out of Freckle's shirt pocket.

"How did you get in there?" Freckle scolded, reaching for the fluffy brown hamster. "Come on, Wrinkles, it's time to go back in your cage. Oh, what's wrong, little fella, are you feeling left out? Feeling like you never get to see the world, stuck in that old cage of yours?" Freckle asked.

"Freckle," Tyler snapped impatiently, "will you stop talking to that hamster and put him in his cage, so we can get going? It's important that we get an early start."

Freckle reluctantly carried Wrinkles upstairs to his room. Once outside, Tyler told Freckle all about the secret code.

"This is so weird," Freckle said. "A real live wizard writing in secret code and living on Dewberry Street." He looked over at Tyler, who was biting on his lip.

"I know it sounds incredible, but it's the

only explanation there is," Tyler said. "You can see the skull for yourself when we stop back at the shop."

"Back? Back at the shop?" Freckle gasped. "Oh, no," he moaned, "not the bike shop. You can't really be serious; you're not going back there, not after all you've told me?"

"We've got to go back, just one more time," Tyler said. "I've got to get my bike. My dad bought me that bike. I couldn't face him if he knew that I'd lost it. You're the only one who can help me, Freck," Tyler pleaded.

"Oh, don't put it like that," Freckle groaned.

"But it's true," Tyler said. "You're my best friend and the only friend I can ask. Come with me one last time. Just one last time."

"But we'll be late for school," Freckle objected.

"We've got an extra ten minutes," Tyler pointed out. "And we won't stay long, just long enough to get the bike back, I promise."

Freckle sighed heavily. "I wonder how long it takes a wizard to turn a boy into a frog," he muttered, as they crossed the street to Wormwood. They ran past the Viking's house as fast as they could and turned the corner to Dew-berry Street. "I don't see anybody in there," Tyler said, when they reached the shop. "And look, there's my note on the cash register, just where I left it. I bet Mr. Quigley hasn't come back yet." Tyler was gazing through the win-dow.

"Oh, great," Freckle moaned, looking down the street, "that means the wizard might show up anytime."

"We're not sure about his being a wizard," Tyler said, his stomach tightening into knots. He stepped up to the door. Please don't let me see the skull, please don't let me see the skull, he thought as he reached for the doorknob. "Come on," he said, pulling Freckle by his jacket sleeve, "we're going in."

The two slowly made their way around the many bicycles. Tyler looked up every now and then, expecting to see Verrocchio overhead. But all he saw were the gently spinning wheels hanging from the ceiling.

What if the old man were in the back room? The thought of talking to him made Tyler's knees wobble.

"Hello," he called out, taking a small step

forward, dragging Freckle with him. "Is anyone back there?" The only reply was the chattering of Freckle's teeth.

"Will you cut that out," Tyler whispered.

"I ca-ca-can't help it," Freckle stammered.
"My teeth always chatter when I'm scared."

"Hello?" Tyler called again, dragging
Freckle a few more steps. The two continued
calling out as they crept along to the back
counter. Tyler pointed to a pile of papers.

"It's under there," he said. "The skull is
right under there. Go ahead and lift up those
papers and you'll see it."

"I don't want to see it!" Freckle exclaimed.
"The only thing I want to see is myself walking
out of this place on two legs. In fact I'd like to
see that right now," he said, turning to leave.

"Oh, no, you don't," Tyler cried, pulling
him back. "You promised you'd help me. I
have to get my bike back, remember?"

"But I don't see it anywhere," Freckle complained.

"It's probably in there," Tyler whispered,
nodding to the heavy velvet curtain leading to
the back room.

"Bu-bu-but what if old Quigley Wizard is back there too?" Freckle croaked.

"Hello, Mr. Quigley," Tyler tried calling once more, "are you back there?" Both boys stood listening, their hearts racing, when suddenly the silence was broken by a noise from the front of the store. Tyler and Freckle both jumped at the sound of the door opening. They raced around the counter to hide. They huddled together, trembling at the sound of each footstep on the old wooden floor. Tyler felt a shiver of goose bumps pop up on his arms. He held his breath.

"I'm too young to be a frog," Freckle whimpered, squeezing Tyler's arm.

"Shh," Tyler whispered, when suddenly he heard a familiar voice.

"Come on out, Tidy Wipe. I know you're in here."

CHAPTER SEVENTEEN

Freckle and Tyler sighed with relief. "It's only the Viking," Tyler said in a low voice.

"I wonder what he's doing here?" Freckle peeked around the counter.

"What kind of bike shop is this? And what are you two doing down there?" snarled the Vike.

Tyler sprang up and tried to stand as tall as he could. He pushed out his chest and threw back his head. He wasn't going to give the Viking the satisfaction of seeing him frightened.

"I told you that it was a special kind of store," Tyler said as calmly as he could. "We were just checking things out for our club."

"Oh, really?" the Viking quipped. "What kind of things?"

"We don't have to explain anything to you," Freckle said.

"No, you don't." The Viking grinned. "But I'll have a lot of explaining to do. I'll have to explain to my club and then maybe the whole school that you two were hiding like two little babies in some old bike shop. What's the matter, babies? Did the big bad bicycles scare you?"

"You want to know what scared us?" Tyler yelled, his voice becoming a high-pitched squeak as he searched through the papers on the counter. "I'll show you what scared us." He reached for the skull and thrust it in the Viking's face.

"Agh! Get that thing out of here!" the Viking screamed, backing away from the counter.

"Oh, so now who's the baby?" Tyler quipped, putting the skull down.

"I don't believe you really picked that thing up," Freckle muttered.

Tyler looked at the skull. He was as astonished as Freckle that he had held it. Even the Viking seemed to be impressed.

"I . . . I saw you two running past my house," he stammered, "and I figured you might be coming here, looking for more stuff for your club, but I never thought you'd be looking for stuff like that. This store is creepy. Why are you hanging around this place anyway?"

"I brought my bike here to get fixed, and we came back to get it," Tyler said. "It must be behind that curtain." He pointed to the long red velvet curtain that hung in front of Quigley's back room.

"You mean the wizard's back room," Freckle added, with a slight chatter of his teeth.

"I'm not snooping around in any wizard's back room," the Viking muttered as he began to walk to the front of the shop.

"What's the matter, Vike," Tyler called, "are you too much of a baby to take a look behind a curtain in some old bike shop?"

The Viking spun around, furious.

"Who are you calling a baby?" he growled.

"You," Tyler replied. "If you're so brave, let's see you come with us behind the curtain and find my bike."

"I'll show you how brave I am," the Viking said, taking a step toward the curtain.

"He can go and get the bike," Freckle whispered in Tyler's ear.

"No," Tyler whispered back, "I've got to

show him once and for all that I have just as much courage as he does. We can do this, Freck. Don't be afraid."

"Oh, I hate it when you start that *we* stuff," Freckle moaned. "Can't I wait here?"

"Alone? With that thing?" Tyler nodded to the skull on the counter.

"On second thought, maybe *we* should stick together," he croaked. They walked over to the Viking, who was standing in front of the curtain. No one spoke as Tyler held up his hand and pulled back the soft velvet material with his fingertips.

It's probably just a little old back room, Tyler tried to tell himself. Just a little old regular room.

The three boys leaned forward, peeking inside. For a minute they stopped breathing.

"This can't be!" Tyler gasped.

"It's like a palace!" Freckle cried.

"Maybe we're dreaming," the Viking whispered.

Tyler blinked several times, but each time he opened his eyes, the same incredible sight stood before him.

The room was huge, more like a hall in a

cathedral. Its stone floor stretched between a row of marble pillars that rose into glistening white arches. Delicately carved alabaster angels held brightly lit torches on the walls, while urns of fresh flowers stood on ornate pedestals below them. One wall was lined with shelves of rainbow-colored glass bottles. Another wall held row after row of leather-bound notebooks.

The early rays of the morning sun were pouring through a large circular window that was fitted with ropes and pulleys. A number of paintings, some draped with white billowing material, were hanging throughout the room by a similar series of ropes. Long wooden tables with heavily carved legs held collections of fossils, rocks, and feathers. A cathedral ceiling rose up in a grand sweep of plaster swirls and curlicues. It was a room out of a palace, out of another time, and yet here it was on Dewberry Street.

"Quentin Quigley must be one powerful wizard!" Tyler exclaimed, his eyes wide with wonder as he stepped onto the smooth stone floor.

CHAPTER EIGHTEEN

The three boys slowly made their way up to a long wooden table covered with a heavily embroidered tapestry. A group of small wax models stood on tiny marble pedestals. There were figures of children running, old men laughing, and women sleeping. Beside the models there were several drawings and an assortment of bones.

"I wonder what kind of witchcraft he uses these bones for?" Tyler asked.

"I don't want to find out," Freckle whimpered. "Get your bike, Ty, just hurry up and get your bike."

As Tyler began to walk away, the Viking called him back.

"Tyler, did you do any more reading for our report last night?"

Tyler couldn't believe his ears. Not only was the Viking using his real name, but he was actually thinking about homework.

"Yeah, I did," Tyler whispered.

"I don't think the wizard is going to be giving us any gold stars for doing our homework," Freckle added. "Come on, let's find the bike and get out of here."

"Wait, you don't understand," the Viking said. "I was reading that library book on Leonardo da Vinci and it said that he used bones for studying anatomy for his artwork," the Viking explained, trying to keep the nervousness out of his voice.

Tyler walked back to the table and took another look.

"Do you see these little statues," the Viking whispered, "and these drawings," he added, pointing to a number of detailed drawings of the human body. "I bet these bones are for studying drawing."

"And look," Tyler exclaimed, "all the writing on these papers is in Mr. Quigley's secret code! In my library book it said that Leonardo da Vinci used a secret code all the time. Mr. Quigley must be a devotee of Leonardo."

"A devotee?" the Viking asked.

"Somebody who really loves Leonardo da Vinci's work," Tyler explained. "That would explain why he made the recorder, just like the one in the library book."

"That's great," Freckle groaned. "Old Quigley Wizard is a devotee. Come on, you guys, let's talk about this somewhere else. Like as far away from here as we can get. Maybe your bike is over there," he said, pointing beyond the table.

"Wow, Vike, look at this," Tyler cried, pointing to a fantastic flying contraption hanging above their heads. It was constructed of wood, with a massive set of wings covered with material and feathers.

"Wha . . . what is it?" Freckle squeaked as the three stood with their heads thrown back and their eyes wide open.

"It's a flying machine," the Viking told him. "Leonardo da Vinci studied flight for years, observing birds and taking all kinds of notes on how they flew and how their wings worked."

"And look at this," Freckle mumbled, stepping up to a large screen that was covered with sketches. "Mr. Quigley must really like horses. He's drawn enough of them."

"Did you say horses?" the Viking cried, rushing over to the screen. "It's Il Cavallo!" he whispered, staring at the incredible drawings of horses, exactly like the ones he and Tyler had seen in the library book.

"This is too weird," Tyler gasped, looking over the drawings. The Viking, meanwhile, was surveying the room once more.

Tyler followed his gaze and their eyes came to rest on the large circular window that was draped with ropes and pulleys. Suddenly Tyler remembered reading about the window that Leonardo da Vinci had invented. Tyler looked at the Viking, whose mouth had dropped open.

"Vike, are you thinking what I'm thinking?" Tyler whispered.

"I'm thinking it," the Viking mumbled, "even though I know it's crazy to be thinking it."

"So, what are you both thinking?" Freckle exclaimed.

Tyler stood back from the screen and his

eyes traveled up to the alabaster angels that hung on the walls.

"Freck, I know it's hard to believe," he began, "but I don't think this is the back room to Quigley's Bicycle Shop."

"No kidding," Freckle snapped. "Anyone can see that it's some kind of wizard's workroom. It's like you said, Quigley is some kind of powerful wizard."

"No, he's not a wizard," the Viking whispered.

"Oh, really? Then what is he?" Freckle wanted to know.

"Do you remember how he told me he was an inventor?" Tyler said. "Well, I think he was telling the truth. I think he's one of the greatest inventors that ever lived. I think he's Leonardo da Vinci," Tyler cried.

"Yeah, right." Freckle smirked. "And I'm Amelia Earhart. Tyler, are you crazy? Leonardo da Vinci lived five hundred years ago."

"Take a look around you," the Viking said. "How old would you say this place is?"

"It does look pretty old," Freckle admitted.

"And here's a sketch of a bicycle," Tyler

said, leaning over a table. "It's just like the sketch in the library book."

"He invented the bicycle?" Freckle asked.

"And the submarine," the Viking told him, pointing to another drawing.

"This is his studio, Freck," Tyler cried. "Leonardo da Vinci's studio! I just know it is. Look, here's his drawing of an army tank! And do you see these tortoiseshells? I read in my library book that he invented the army tank after studying the shells of turtles." Tyler reached down and picked up one of the large shells that sat beside the drawing. "Leonardo da Vinci studied nature to see how things work," he exclaimed, tapping his knuckle on the hard shell. "That way he could dream up new things!"

"But if he died almost five hundred years ago, how could he be here now?" Freckle wanted to know.

Tyler bit down on his lip. "To go beyond time," he mumbled aloud. "That's it! He invented so many different things, maybe he invented a time machine!"

"Are you saying that he invented a machine that could transport him, and his workshop, from century to century?" the Viking asked.

Freckle shook his head. "That's why the building was in the air! He must have been using his time machine to transport it to Dewberry Street."

"The label on one of the bicycles said 1894," Tyler whispered. "I wonder if the shop came from that year. That would explain why the bicycles are so old but look so new. He must have stopped some place in 1894 and decided to take the shop with him."

"But why?" Freckle wondered aloud.

"Maybe because he loves bicycles," the Viking suggested. "He did invent them years ago."

Everyone grew quiet as the muffled sound of bells tinkled in the distance. Tyler's eyes darted to the curtain.

"The door!" he gasped. "I think someone just opened the door to the bike shop!" Another wave of goose bumps swept up Tyler's arms as he listened to the heavy footsteps beyond the curtain.

CHAPTER NINETEEN

The three boys froze, not knowing what to do. The thought of facing Leonardo da Vinci was overwhelming.

"Quick, hide," Tyler cried, as he lifted the tapestry that hung down over a table and dove underneath. Freckle and the Viking dove in behind him. They waited in silence, listening to the muffled sounds coming from the bike shop. Then without warning, a loud squeak erupted from Freckle's jacket. Tyler looked over to see Wrinkles's tiny pink nose and whiskers twitching as he peeked over the edge of Freckle's pocket.

"What's he doing here?" Tyler cried.

Freckle gave out a little groan and gently pushed the hamster's head back into the jacket pocket. "I couldn't help it," Freckle admitted.

"Wrinkles looked so depressed this morning. He never gets out. I thought he could use a little excitement. You know, like a field trip."

Tyler shook his head. "This is turning out to be one exciting field trip. I hope his little heart can take it all."

"I hope *my* little heart can take it," the Viking moaned, as the footsteps beyond the curtain grew louder.

"Hey, Ty," Freckle whispered, "if Leonardo da Vinci invented a time machine, that means he's not a wizard, right?"

"Right," Tyler mumbled, as Verrocchio squawked loudly.

"And so he can't turn us into frogs, right?" Freckle said.

"Right," Tyler answered as calmly as he could.

"Unless," the Viking added.

"Unless?" Freckle repeated anxiously.

"Unless he invented a machine that can turn boys into frogs," the Viking replied in a husky whisper. On hearing this, Tyler's goose bumps multiplied, Wrinkles let out another squeak, and Freckle's teeth began to chatter all over again.

As they sat huddled together, Tyler turned to look at the Viking. It had been awhile since he had seen him sneer or heard him snarl. The Viking was almost beginning to look normal.

"So, Verrocchio, you are anxious to leave." The melodic voice of the old man suddenly echoed through the great room. Freckle held his hand over Wrinkles's head to muffle his squeaks, while Tyler held his hand over Freckle's mouth to muffle the sound of his chattering teeth. The Viking's face had gone white as flour and he looked as if he were about to cry.

"So many wonderful machines," Tyler heard the old man mutter as he approached the table. "Computing machines, washing machines, talking machines, hair-drying machines, traveling machines. And what were those incredible machines filled with moving images called?" Verrocchio squawked loudly as he landed on the table over their heads.

"Ah, yes, Verrocchio, now I remember— they are called televisions. Amazing! Simply amazing." The old man sighed. "Such a time to live in, eh, old friend? Think of it, no longer do people travel by horse. They now have airplanes, trains, and automobiles. Everything happens so much faster in this time. Even their meals are speeded up with the invention of the microwave. I would love to bring one home with us, but can you imagine what people of our time would say if they saw us 'nuking' our dinner?" The old man chuckled. "We'd be branded as wizards for sure, and besides I really didn't take a liking to this food called 'nuked popcorn,' he muttered, as he opened a bag of popcorn and threw some down on the table.

"Nuked corn . . . eee . . . nuked some corn, eee," Verrocchio screeched, pecking at the popcorn.

"You don't agree with me, eh? Well, you'd better not get accustomed to it," the old man said, walking across the room. "There won't even be such a thing as a microwave at home for another five hundred years. Ah, Firenze, I must admit I'm homesick. We have stayed far too long, though it has improved our English, wouldn't you say?"

"Much improved . . . much improved," the parrot chirped.

"Um, and so many amazing machines, yet the most amazing machine of all is still unknown to them," the old man said softly.

Tyler and the Viking peeked out from under the table, but Freckle was too petrified to move. The old man was standing before a large wood-paneled wall that was heavily decorated with carvings. Three long rope tassels hung down in the center. The old man gave one of the tassels a yank. To Tyler's amazement, the entire wall lifted up, revealing a small hidden room lit with torches. In the center a giant cube shimmered in the torchlight. The cube was a little taller than the old man. It was covered with hundreds of tiny mirrored squares. In the middle of the cube was a small wooden door with a tiny marble handle. On top of the cube, a nine-pointed star twinkled and sparkled.

"Oh, my gosh, do you think that's the time machine?" the Viking asked. "I read about his last invention in my library book," he continued. "It said that Leonardo was using all kinds of mirrors, and he had grown so secretive, no one knew what he was inventing."

"I've never seen a time machine," Tyler admitted, "but that thing looks strange enough to be one."

"I want to go home," Freckle whimpered, hanging his head. Wrinkles nuzzled his nose.

Tyler peeked again at the old man. He was walking toward the shimmering cube. He opened the small door in the cube's center.

"Wow," Tyler gasped as a small painted canvas stared out at them. Tyler instantly recognized the faint smile of the woman in the painting.

"It's her!" he gasped. "Take a look, Vike. It's the Mona Lisa!"

"It is her!" the Viking whispered.

"Then that must really be him," Tyler added. "Do you believe it? We're looking at Leonardo da Vinci!"

"Whatever you say, Ty," Freckle mumbled. "But isn't the Mona Lisa in a museum somewhere?"

"Maybe the one in the museum is a fake," Tyler whispered.

"Or maybe he painted two versions," the Viking added. The old man stood in front of the painting with his arms outstretched.

"Ah, *cara mia,*" he said softly, "with your

eyes, how much have I seen! And it does my heart good to see so many of my inventions finally being developed. The bicycle, for instance, that was a wonderful surprise. I was so excited when I came upon Quigley's shop that I decided to borrow it for the rest of my journey. I suppose it is time to return it." He stepped up to the mirrored cube.

"What's he doing now?" Freckle wanted to know.

Tyler leaned forward to get a better view. "It's hard to see," he muttered, pressing close to the Viking.

Both boys grew quiet as they heard the old man exclaim, "Now, we are ready to begin the return journey!" They watched as he stepped back. "Come, Verrocchio," he called. "Stay close, my friend, we've a long way to travel!" Verrocchio spread his brilliant green wings and flew across the room to his master, landing on his shoulder.

"Oh, no," Tyler moaned, as he watched the star on the top of the cube being to spin. Suddenly a loud hissing noise filled the air and a bright light shot out of the Mona Lisa's eyes!

his nose on his sleeve.
. "It was your idea to
said. "You got us into
et us out."
don't want to go out
tted. "If Leonardo da
e and we've discovered
t let us stay in our own

at chance," the Viking
g sound from the cube
ou want to end up like

m to turn off the ma-

e, right," Tyler said.
arguing and besides,
ook a deep breath and
from under the table
ng noise above them.
ottles were clinking.
ble.
cried, "go out and tell
ine! You've got to stop

"Travel?" Freckle cried, tugging on Tyler's leg. "Did he say, 'A long way to travel'?"

Tyler's hands got clammy and a new wave of goose bumps popped out on his skin.

"It does sound like he's going somewhere," he whispered, looking at the Viking and Freckle. Their eyes had become as big as silver dollars.

CHAPTER TWENTY

"If Leonardo da Vinci came to Dewberry Street with his studio," Freckle cried, "he'll probably leave with it! And with us too! Tyler you've got to stop him!"

Tyler was about to answer when Wrinkles let out his loudest squeak yet. In a daring move, the fluffy hamster leaped out of Freckle's pocket, landing on the floor with a thud. Freckle tried scooping him up, but Wrinkles was moving too fast. His tiny claws scraped the hard stones as he scrambled out of Freckle's reach. In a matter of seconds, the hamster had raced out from under the table and was heading straight for the secret chamber.

"Wrinkles, no!" Freckle gasped as the frightened hamster stood beneath the gaze o

kles," he said, wiping

The Viking frowned
come here, Tyler," he
this, now you should g

Tyler squirmed. "I
there alone," he admi
Vinci realizes we're her
his secret, he might no
time."

"We'll have to take th
reasoned, as the hissin
grew louder. "Unless y
Wrinkles."

"You've got to get h
chine," Freckle said.

"Turn off the machi
He knew it was no use
there was no time. He t
was about to step out
when he heard a rattli
Papers were shaking,
The table began to tren

"Hurry, Ty," Freckle
him to turn off the mach
him!"

The room was filling with a golden light. With each revolution of the cube, the light streaming out of the painting's eyes grew brighter. Everything seemed to be shimmering in its path, shaking under its brilliance. Tyler's knees buckled as he climbed out from under the jittery table. His heart was pumping in his ears. He closed his eyes tight, but under the painting's golden gaze, his eyelids seemed tissue-paper thin. The light poured through them as if they had never been closed.

"Ty, wha-wha- what's hap . . ." Freckle's faint cry sounded as if it were miles away. Tyler wanted to open his mouth and call to his friend, but instead he stood still as a statue, his body as unmovable as marble. An invisible weight pressed against him, and Tyler wondered if he was still breathing.

Then everything seemed to come to a grinding stop, caught in the grip of some unseen force, yet at the same time moving, moving at lightning speed. The hissing noise turned into a high-pitched whistle that tickled Tyler's ears and somewhere, just beyond the whistle, he thought he heard the tinkling of bells, or was he imagining it? He struggled to move, but instead stood motionless in motion, staring through closed eyes into the brilliant golden beam and the mysterious smile of the Mona Lisa.

CHAPTER TWENTY-ONE

And then everything was as it had been. The light from the painting's eyes faded, and the cube came to a sudden stop. Tyler's breath returned, he stretched his fingers and arched his back. He could move again. As he stood blinking, he caught sight of the old man, who was slowly turning in his direction. Tyler sank to his knees and ducked under the table, behind the tapestry, before the old man could see him.

"Wha- What happened?" Freckle whispered, his eyes glassy and his face a sheet of white under his many freckles. The Viking also looked stunned.

"Do you think we went anywhere?" Freckle whimpered.

"Naw," the Viking tried to reassure him,

but his voice was far too jittery to be reassuring.

"The Vike's right," Tyler said, his voice just as jittery. "The old man was probably warming the machine up." The three boys could hear footsteps approaching. Tyler peeked out to see the old man go padding by in his pointed leather slippers, the ends of his long green robe gliding over the smooth gray stones. He was carrying a bag of microwaved popcorn and the parrot was still perched on his shoulder.

"Ah, Verrocchio, how is it possible for one man to be so absentminded?" the old man muttered. "I forgot to return the little one's bicycle to him. That will never do. I'm afraid I'd make a dreadful shopkeeper," he chuckled, reaching up to offer Verrocchio a piece of popcorn to nibble. "Now, where did I put that bicycle? It won't take me but a few minutes to slip that repaired chain back on." Tyler watched as the old man walked under the arches and disappeared behind a series of screens.

"This is our chance to make a run for it," the Viking said.

"Right," Tyler agreed. "If we hurry, we can run out through the bike shop."

"But what about Wrinkles?" Freckle cried. "I can't leave without Wrinkles."

"Wrinkles has already left, Freck," Tyler said softly. "There isn't a lot we can do about that now. Come on," he whispered, taking hold of Freckle's arm, "we've got to hurry."

They cautiously climbed out from under the table and raced for the curtain. As Tyler reached for the velvet material, he could hear the old man moving behind the screen. With a sweep of his arm, Tyler threw the material to the side and all three boys bounded into the old bicycle shop. They were halfway across the store when Tyler tripped and fell over a bicycle wheel. He quickly got up and raced for the door, joining Freckle and the Viking in front of the shop.

"What are you doing?" Tyler cried. "Don't stop here. Let's run home."

"Home?" the Viking murmured, staring down the street. "I think we'd have to do a lot more than run to get home!"

Tyler followed his gaze. "This can't be Dew-

berry Street," he gasped, looking at the cobblestones that had replaced the street's
blacktop. There was a loud clip-clopping of
hooves as horses and carriages trotted by. The
familiar wide cement sidewalks were now
nothing more than muddy paths that lined the
street.

Tyler watched as two women in long skirts
and bonnets, their eyes cast down, carefully
maneuvered their way around the horse dung
that seemed to be everywhere. Its sweet pun-
gent scent hung over the street like a cloud.

Freshly painted white-and-green storefronts
faced each other up and down the road. Red-
and-blue-striped awnings hung cheerfully over
large display windows etched in gold paint.
Three young boys in knickers and caps were
running down a path across the street. They
were carrying sticks and had large hoops slung
over their shoulders. A pack of older boys followed them. They were laughing and spitting
onto the cobblestones, but they quieted down
when they saw the three strange figures standing in front of Quigley's Bicycle Shop.

"I guess we did go somewhere," Tyler mumbled, looking up and down the street. "Somewhere into the past!"

"Yeah, look at the man on the bicycle across the street," Freckle cried. "It's the same bicycle we saw in Quigley's shop."

"And the year on the bike said 1894," Tyler gasped. "Do you remember when Leonardo was talking about finding Quigley's Bicycle Shop? He must have landed with his studio in 1894 and then taken the shop along with him to the future."

"He also said it was time to return the shop," the Viking added. "If Quigley's came from 1894, Leonardo would have to return it to 1894."

"I feel sick," Freckle moaned.

"It's all so different," Tyler said, unable to take his eyes off the scene before him. He turned to look back at the shop. "He did say that he was going to return the bike, didn't he?" Tyler muttered. "Come on," he cried, shaking himself, "if Leonardo's on his way to returning my bike, he'll be leaving with the bike shop any minute!"

Tyler and the Viking turned on their heels

and headed back into the shop. Freckle was right behind them until he heard a loud, "Squeak, squeak, squeak."

"Wrinkles!" Freckle cried. A group of big boys, at least a head taller than the Viking, was approaching from the other side of the street. They looked menacing as they strutted up to the shop and stood eyeing the strange intruders.

"Freck, come on," Tyler called nervously from the doorway. "You don't want to get stuck here, do you?"

"Ty, look at the one in the middle," Freckle whispered. A big red-faced boy with a crop of carroty hair and a flattened nose was standing barefoot. From his shirt pocket a pair of little black eyes and a pink nose with whiskers was sticking out.

"It's Wrinkles, Ty, it's really him," Freckle cried, taking a step toward the boy.

"Who are you and why are you dressed in those funny clothes?" the boy asked.

"It's a long story," Freckle began, taking another step. "You've got my hamster in your pocket, and I'd like him back."

"What? This funny mouse?" the boy said with a shake of his carroty curls. "I found him fair and square and now he belongs to me. I'm going to play with him for a bit and then I'll pitch him in the river. Ever see a mouse try and do the backstroke?" He laughed. All the other boys laughed with him.

"Please don't hurt him," Freckle pleaded. "Wrinkles isn't wild. He's a pet."

"Wrinkles, Wrinkles, Wrinkles," the group sang out, as the boy pulled Wrinkles out of his pocket and threw him into the air. The terrified hamster squeaked with horror as he fell back into the boy's hands.

"Stop that!" Freckle yelled.

"Says who?" the red-faced boy called out.

"Says me," the Viking bellowed in his huskiest heavyweight voice, stepping out of the bicycle shop. He narrowed his eyes and puckered his mouth, assuming the bully pose that Tyler knew so well. A few of the smaller boys fell away from the group, but no one else budged.

"And just who do you think you are?" asked an older hulk of a boy. He spit on the ground, his face a hard, mean mask. It was bully against bully, only one bully was much bigger and meaner looking than the other.

Another big boy gave the Viking a hard shove, making him step backward.

"Leave my friend alone," Tyler yelled. The Viking looked up, surprised.

"And just who do you think you are?" the mean-faced bully demanded.

Tyler gulped. "I'm a wizard," he said.

CHAPTER TWENTY-TWO

"A wizard?" the bully repeated with a smirk.

"Yes, that's why I'm dressed this way," Tyler explained. Then he reached into his back pocket and pulled out his pocket calculator. All the boys in the pack leaned closer to get a look.

"What's that?" the bully asked.

"It's . . . it's . . ." Tyler stood, trying to think of a good answer. "It's a wizard's weapon. A . . . a . . . death ray globulon gun," he said with a grin.

"That doesn't look like any gun that I've ever seen," one of the boys in the crowd called out.

"Well, that's because you've probably never seen a wizard's gun before," Tyler explained.

"Where are the bullets?" another boy wanted to know.

"It doesn't have bullets," Tyler told him as a line of sweat formed on his upper lip. "It has invisible death rays." He pushed down on the *on* button and a faint beep went off. Everyone jumped back. Tyler's face had become dark and serious. "It has a lot of magic power," he said with a frown.

"You can't fool us," the thick-necked bully growled, grabbing Tyler by the collar of his jacket and lifting him up off the ground. "Does this look like a wizard to you?" he yelled to the crowd of boys. They hooted with laughter. "These three are all done up in these funny-looking clothes 'cause they probably just left the boat. I bet they ain't even Americans." This last remark produced an onslaught of jeers and catcalls from the crowd. "And do you know what I'm thinking?" he continued in his rough gravelly voice. "I'm thinking that being foreigners, they probably need a bath." With this he lowered Tyler over a mound of horse dung, streaking his sneakers with manure. "Hmm, he's a stinking foreigner, all right."

A cheer went up from the crowd as the boys

grabbed hold of Freckle and the Viking. "To the river! To the river!" the crowd sang out. Tyler's eyes darted to the bicycle shop. He knew that the old man would be activating the time machine any second. They had no time to spare.

"Wait!" Tyler screamed as loud as he could. "We're not foreigners. We're wizards. And I can prove it!"

At this remark, the bully lowered him to the ground. "All right," he called out, letting go of his collar, "go ahead, then, and use that gobbledygook gun of yours and show us just how powerful a wizard you are." Tyler turned to Freckle and the Viking, not knowing what to say next. He cleared his throat and coughed, but the bully could see that he was stalling. The bully grabbed his collar again and was about to yank Tyler into the air when a loud hissing noise wove its way out of the bicycle shop's door. Everyone turned around to see the building begin to tremble.

"Hey! What's going on?" the bully cried, dropping Tyler to the ground and backing away from him. Everyone stood stunned at the sight of the wobbly building.

"I told you we were wizards," Tyler cried. "Quick, Freck. Come on, Vike," he called, pushing his way through the crowd. He ran to the shop's door and slipped through. "Leonardo must have activated the time machine. Hurry!" The boys on the street stood dumbfounded as they watched the building begin to gently sway back and forth. The Viking threw himself into the shop's doorway. Freckle was about to follow him when he turned around.

"Freck, quick, get in here," Tyler screamed.

"I can't," Freckle cried. "I can't leave Wrinkles behind." The hissing noise was growing louder by the minute. Tyler bit down on his lip and then held up his pocket calculator. He aimed it at the terrified group of boys who were huddled together on the cobblestones.

"They *are* wizards!" a smaller boy cried, falling to the ground and covering his head with his hands.

"Don't any of you move," Tyler ordered, waving the calculator in front of them. "I don't want to have to use this," he yelled, pushing the on button again and activating the beep. "Give us Wrinkles now, or I'll use the death ray on all of you!"

"Give him the mouse, Jim, give him the mouse!" a number of terrified boys cried out. The hissing noise turned into a loud whistle as the shop's windows began to rattle. Tyler and the Viking had gotten hold of the back of Freckle's jacket and were trying to pull him through the doorway. Suddenly a bright beam of light shone through the velvet curtain, filling the shop with a golden glow.

Tyler struggled to hang on to Freckle. "Freck, hurry!" Tyler cried as he felt a gripping paralysis slowly overtake him.

CHAPTER TWENTY-THREE

The frightened bully named Jim grabbed Wrinkles and threw him to Freckle, who caught him before falling into the shop on top of Tyler and the Viking. The door slammed shut as the boys heard the tinkling of bells and a whistling sound in their ears. Everything became a blur of golden light. Tyler experienced the same strange sensation of being held fast while moving at lightning speed. He struggled to open his mouth, but it was useless. He tried to blink his eyes, but they were as heavy as lead.

Then, quite suddenly, everything returned to normal. "Get your foot off my ear," the Viking moaned.

"Get your elbow out of my stomach," Tyler groaned.

"Whose arm is this?" Freckle asked groggily.

"Squeak, squeak, squeak!" Wrinkles complained, as his nose picked up the scent of Tyler's sneakers.

"That was close," the Viking sighed, looking at Tyler. "I've got to hand it to you, though. That gobbledygook story was great. You're pretty smart for a litt . . ., er, for a kid."

"Thanks, Vike," Tyler said. "And you're pretty nice for a Viking."

"I wonder what year we're in now?" Freckle said, getting to his feet. Tyler was about to investigate when a loud screech filled the air.

"Company's come . . . eee . . . company's come . . . eee." The velvet curtain was pulled to the side and Verrocchio flew into the shop. The old man followed close behind him.

"Ah, little one!" the familiar voice called. The old man smiled impishly as he pushed Tyler's bicycle over the old floorboards.

"Come back for your bicycle, have you? I trust that you'll find the workmanship satisfactory," he said, pointing to the repaired chain. Tyler gulped. "At Quigley's we pride ourselves on our fine workmanship."

I'm talking to somebody who was born over five hundred years ago! Tyler thought frantically. I'm talking to Leonardo da Vinci! What do I say? But the old man's bright eyes and soft smile made Tyler's fear slip away. To him the old man would always be Quentin Quigley, the strange old Quentin Quigley who loved bicycles, flutes, and rainbows.

"Thanks, Mr. Quigley," Tyler grinned shyly, reaching for the handlebars.

"Such a fine morning for a ride," the old man said as he opened the shop's door. The three boys could see the old familiar Dewberry Street stretching out beyond the door.

"It's Dewberry Street!" Tyler gasped.

"Our Dewberry Street!" Freckle sighed. The Viking flashed his big-toothed grin as they looked out over the modern black asphalt and the wide cement sidewalks.

"Come," the old man beckoned, stepping out of the shop. "And please don't forget that we aren't ready for our grand opening, so Quigley's Bicycle Shop will be our little secret, yes?" His dark eyes flashed hypnotically under his raised silver eyebrows.

"Yes," Tyler, Freckle, and the Viking replied together. Tyler pushed his bicycle through the open door onto the sidewalk, while his two friends rushed out behind him. As soon as their sneakers hit the sidewalk, Freckle and the Viking were off and running. Tyler watched them duck behind a Dumpster. He felt a warm, comfortable feeling spread over him as he looked down the familiar empty street with its worn dilapidated buildings. The old man stood beside him, his eyes twinkling merrily.

"I am so glad that I had the opportunity to meet you, Maestro Harrison," he said with a smile. Tyler felt a pang of sadness, since he knew that the old man was saying good-bye.

"But I haven't paid you for the chain, and I haven't any money with me," Tyler protested. "Can't I come back tomorrow?"

"There is no need, little one. At Quigley's we often accept payment in the form of a trade."

"But I didn't give you anything in trade," Tyler protested.

"On the contrary, your song was payment enough," the old man told him.

"My song?" Tyler didn't understand until

the old man threw back his head and began to whistle the first few bars of "Mississippi Hotcakes."

"Eee . . . time waits for no man . . . eee . . . time waits for no man . . . not even Quigley . . . " Verrocchio interrupted with a screech. The old man stroked his beard and shook his head.

"I'm afraid that my old friend, Verrocchio, is correct. And so I must return to my work. One has little time for rest in the bicycle business. It's all about travel, you see," he said with a wink.

"It must be a big challenge, being in the business of travel," Tyler said softly.

"Ah, but we know something about dealing with challenges, don't we?" the old man said, gently rapping his knuckles on Tyler's forehead. "Yes, it's a challenging business, the travel business, but do you know the best part?" He bent down and cupped his hand to his mouth. "It's the repeat customers," he whispered in Tyler's ear.

"But how do they find you?" Tyler frowned.

"They don't have to. We find them. At Quigley's we never forget a good customer." The old man straightened his back and looked up the street. "Your friends are waiting, little one. You had better run along, or you'll be late for school."

"School! Oh, my gosh!" Tyler cried. "I forgot all about school."

"Off with you, then." The old man chuckled and waved his hand.

Tyler turned his bike around and began to pedal toward the Dumpster. Together the three friends headed up Dewberry Street, talking and laughing in the bright morning light. When they came to the end of the sidewalk, Tyler turned around to wave, but the door to Quigley's Bicycle Shop was closed.

CHAPTER TWENTY-FOUR

Mrs. Bailey was putting math problems on the board as Tyler, Freckle, and the Vike snuck into the classroom. "Today is a special day," Mrs. Bailey was saying with her back to the class. "Mr. Nutley will be coming to observe our class, along with some student teachers." (Mr. Nutley was the school's principal.)

As the three boys tiptoed to their seats, the other students in the class began to whisper. Danny Featherman threw a spitball, Michael Miller threw an eraser, and Marc Freer let out a series of low hoots. Mrs. Bailey turned around to see what all the commotion was about just as Tyler sank into his seat. He looked over to see that Freckle and the Vike were seated too. At that moment Mr. Nutley and the two student teachers walked through the door. Smiling broadly, Mrs. Bailey welcomed them to the class. Mr. Nutley introduced the student teachers, and then Mrs. Bailey led them all to the empty chairs that were set up in the back of the room.

As they passed Tyler's desk, Mr. Nutley looked down and his nose began to twitch. Mr. Nutley was a heavyset man with a red face and a bald head. Tyler fidgeted, trying to smile, but Mr. Nutley didn't smile back. His red face was all puckered up as if he had just sucked on a lemon. He stood staring down at Tyler's manure-streaked sneakers.

Mrs. Bailey, seeing the principal stop at Tyler's desk (and seeing Tyler sitting at his desk), double-checked her attendance sheet for the day. She scanned the room and frowned on seeing Freckle and the Viking in their seats too.

"Tyler Harrison, Jay Kosa, and Michael Beidelman, please come up to my desk," she ordered. As they marched up to the front of the room, Mr. Nutley followed them, his nose still twitching.

"Would you mind explaining why you three were late for school today?" Mrs. Bailey asked.

"And where is it that you've been?" Mr. Nutley added, pointing down to Tyler's sneakers. Tyler squirmed uneasily. He looked at Freckle and the Vike. They were squirming too.

"The Vike . . . er Michael and I were doing some extra research for our history project on Leonardo da Vinci," Tyler said truthfully.

"And I was helping them," Freckle quickly added. Mr. Nutley's eyebrows shot up.

"The three of you were doing research on Leonardo da Vinci and that's why you're late for school? Is that correct?" He looked at Tyler suspiciously.

"Yes, Mr. Nutley," Tyler replied. The principal turned to the Viking.

"Yes, Mr. Nutley," the Viking said, nodding his head. Mr. Nutley turned to Freckle.

"Yes Mr. . . . Squeak! Squeak! Squeak!" The principal's eyes grew as big as saucers as Wrinkles leaped from Freckle's pocket and onto Mrs. Bailey's desk. From there he streaked to the chalkboard ledge as Freckle tried to catch him. Soon the entire class was up and out of their seats chasing the runaway hamster. Even the two student teachers joined in the chase.

Tyler, Freckle, and the Viking were punished with three weeks of no recess and they each had to write Mr. Nutley and the student teachers an apology for having interrupted their visit. Wrinkles was assigned to the old rabbit cage in the back of the room, and Tyler was ordered to take off his sneakers and leave them in the hall for the remainder of the day. After that, things settled down, and Tyler found himself almost enjoying the luxury of walking around the classroom in his stocking feet.

When the last bell finally rang, Tyler and the Vike waited for Freckle, who was packing up Wrinkles in the pocket of his backpack. Then the three friends took off as fast as they could.

They didn't speak as they walked toward the far end of Dewberry Street. Quigley's Bicycle

Shop was gone. In its place was an empty lot, littered with trash and bits of broken glass. Everything was gone. The big display window, the many shining bicycles, the old man, the parrot, it had all vanished. The only thing that remained was the crumbling stone foundation, where a building had once rested.

Tyler felt a lump in his throat. He walked over and sank down on a smooth block of stone. He stared at the withered crabgrass and bits of broken glass. The wind blew a tear from his eye. A crumpled piece of candy wrapper tumbled by his foot.

"I wonder where he's off to now," Freckle whispered, looking up to the sky. Tyler followed his gaze and saw a large bird gracefully gliding overhead.

"It's like it was never even here," the Viking said, picking up a stone and throwing it across the lot. Tyler fought back tears as he searched the sky for a hint of color, a trace of a rainbow. But there was none. He sat with his eyes closed, remembering the old man's voice and his shop full of wonderful bicycles. He remembered the sad sweet recorder, Verrocchio's loud squawking, the old man gently knocking on his head. He could hear the melodic voice. "Things are not always what they seem."

He's right, Tyler thought. Things aren't always what they seem. Quigley's Bicycle Shop was so much more than just a bicycle shop. Tyler looked over at the Viking, who was kicking an old rusted can.

And the Vike, he thought. Even the Vike is different. I always thought that he was a big bully who didn't care about anyone else. I never thought he could be a friend of mine. Tyler smiled. I guess I'm not the person he thought I was either. He probably thought I was just some little wimp; gosh, I even thought I was a wimp.

"Things are not always what they seem," Tyler mumbled aloud. He lifted his fist to his forehead and knocked several times. Looking up to the clear autumn sky, he began to imagine a thin line of color, a glimmer of red, a hint of orange, the warm flush of gold. And soon in his imagination the horizon was streaked with a blaze of different colors, one more brilliant than the next. The entire sky had become one huge magnificent rainbow!

"Anybody wanna come over to my house

and see how my grandma's mustache remover works?" Tyler suddenly heard someone ask. He looked over and saw Danny Featherman standing on the sidewalk. "What are you guys doing hanging out here, anyway?" Danny wanted to know.

"We were just leaving, weren't we, Ty?" Freckle said, kicking an empty can. Tyler blinked and looked back up to the clear blue sky.

"Yeah," he said, jumping off the stone block, "we were just leaving."

"So what's this about your grandma's mustache?" Freckle asked as he and Danny crossed the street. Tyler walked out to the sidewalk and turned to take one last look at the empty lot. The Viking came up and stood beside him.

"Good-bye, Quigley's Bicycle Shop," Tyler said softly.

"It looks like it was never here," the Viking mumbled. "Almost like we imagined it or something."

"Oh, it was here, all right," Tyler whispered. "I know it was here." The two started